Big Girls Do It

JASINDA WILDER

*To Cara,
Do it girl!
♂ Jasinda Wilder*

This is a work of fiction. Names, characters, places, and incidents are either the product of the author's imagination or are used fictitiously. Any resemblance to actual events, places, organizations, or persons, whether living or dead, is entirely coincidental.

BIG GIRLS DO IT

ISBN: 978-0-9882642-4-3
Copyright © 2012 by Jasinda Wilder

Contents

To Chase and Jeff for all the lessons and love

Big Girls Do It Better

TWO THINGS GET ME INTO TROUBLE: food, and my mouth. That's how it all started with Chase: first food, then my mouth. I had just finished DJing at a bar appropriately called The Dive, and I needed a snack. I headed to the twenty-four-hour Ram's Horn a few miles away from the bar.

That night, I was way more sober than I usually was whenever I visited the Ram's Horn. Let's just say the tips at The Dive were usually of the liquid variety, but that particular night, I hadn't been tipped as well as usual. Still, I'd had a couple, and I swayed as I made my way through the crowded parking lot. I stumbled through the door and bumped right into trouble of the tall, dark, and handsome variety. He apologized as I looked away, flushing in embarrassment.

I sneaked a peek, and embarrassment turned to lust. This guy was HOT. I couldn't make myself meet his eyes. I mumbled an apology and scurried to my usual corner booth, where I hid behind the menu.

I pretended to peruse a menu I knew by heart. I've always had a passion for life, and that translated into overindulgence. What can I say? I've never met a cupcake I didn't want to get to know better.

I was still staring at the menu when he came over. He was so sexy, even his pants were sexy.

"Can I sit with you?" His voice was like a mellow, throbbing bass line.

Anything you want, Mr. Sexypants, I thought. I blushed scarlet from my forehead all the way down to my ample cleavage.

"Sure," I mumbled, acting like I didn't care either way.

I looked up at him again, and he was twice as sexy as he'd been ten seconds before. I wanted to say something cool, but in my tipsy state, I could barely focus, and my menu kept shifting between single and double images.

Mr. Sexypants ordered water, because he was just that cool. I thought about ordering salad, so I could be cool, too, but when the waitress came and I actually opened up my mouth, I said "Lemon pie."

Pie? Really? *Awesome job, Anna*, I scolded myself.

I played with my hair, twisting a lock of my bottle-blonde hair between my fingers. It smelled like smoke.

"You seem like you know your way around this place," Mr. Sexypants said.

"No, not really," I lied. "I actually DJ down the street at The Dive."

Why did I just tell him where I work?

"You're a DJ?"

"Yeah. I also sing and play music at a few local bars."

"Oh, you sing," he said, flashing his absurdly straight and white teeth at me. "I'm a singer, too."

Of course Mr. Sexypants would be a singer.

"Really?" I said. "Like at church?"

"No, in a band. We're called 6 Feet Tall. We just got back from playing at CBGB's in New York."

The waitress brought our food, I think. She must have, since food had appeared and I was eating it.

I smiled, ate my lemon pie, and twirled my hair again. *Is this actually happening to me right now?* I put my hand down on my leg and pinched myself. Yep, really happening.

I glanced down, more to get away from Mr. Sexypants and his fiery brown eyes than anything else, and that was when I remembered what I was wearing: knee-high black hooker boots, fish-net stockings, and a size-eighteen sequined leopard-print dress. I went ten shades of scorching red all over again.

"How's the pie?" he asked, still with that too-damn-cute smirk. He knew exactly what he was doing to me, and he was enjoying watching me squirm.

"Uh...great, thanks." I scarfed down the last couple bites. "I really need to get going."

"The pie is on me," he said. "I was lonely, sitting all by myself. My name is Chase, by the way."

"Nice to meet you Chase. I'm Anna." I shook his hand, trying desperately to ignore the sparks of heat that ran up my arm at the touch of his strong, calloused fingers. "Good luck with your band."

With that, I scooted my butt out of the booth and into my car as quick as I could. I turned the key in my car and looked at the clock: three thirty-eight am. I needed to get home before my roommate Jamie started calling the police to look for my dead body. She hated my job and was always worried guys were going to attack me as I was leaving the bar. I've tried explaining to her several times that serial killers don't kill fat girls. I turned to check for a car before I started to pull out, but jammed the brakes when the passenger-side door opened.

"I didn't want to let you go without getting your

phone number." Chase's bass-line voice washed over me from the open door.

"My mother taught me not to give my phone number to strange men."

"So I'm strange, now, huh?" He shot me the smirk again.

"You know what I meant. I don't know you." It took all my control to keep my voice even.

"What if I want to get to know you?" He smiled at me again, and I swear I forgot what my name was.

And then he kissed me. Not a tiny, friendly, introductory kiss, either; it was a deep, almost-tongues-touching kiss. A soul-scorching kiss. My foot slid off the brake and the car started rolling, and he had to jump out of the way to avoid being run over.

"Sorry about that," I mumbled, trying not to touch my lips where his had just been.

"I'll see you again, Anna. Real soon." He shut the car door before I could finish mumbling, "Good night."

He smiled at me as he turned to jog back to the restaurant.

He swaggered into The Dive the following week, wearing tight leather pants and a sleeveless black T-shirt. It was a look not many men could have pulled off, but he wore it like he'd invented

it. I mean, damn, those pants hugged his ass like a
second skin, and his arms were brawny, bulging,
and writhing with gorgeous tattoos. He was lean
in the hips, wide in the shoulders, and...

I was completely screwed.

That was before he picked up the mic. He let a
few others go first, some not-quite-drunk regulars
who had decent voices, people I could rely on to
get the night started. Chase picked "All I Want"
by Toad the Wet Sprocket. He took the mic in one
hand, curled the cord around the other, standing
with his weight on one foot, head down, tapping a
toe to the opening notes. Most people, when waiting for their song to start, glance at their table of
friends for encouragement, or stare with nervous
eyes at the prompter, waiting for the lyrics to start
turning blue.

Chase milked the moment like a true performer.
He drew everyone's eyes, and he knew it; rather
than just waiting for the cue to start singing, he
was building tension, making sure every eye was
on him. The music shifted from the intro to the
first verse, and Chase lifted the mic to his mouth,
drew a deep breath...and blew me away. The man
could sing. He worked the crowd, getting those
who knew the song to join in on the chorus, got the
rest clapping and trying to sing along. He turned
a dingy dive bar into a concert hall before his first
number was over.

Of course, at the time, all I could see was his glorious body and smooth skin. All I could feel was the rush of pure desire coursing through my body to gather in a damp pool between my thighs. I remembered the heat and pressure of his lips on mine one week ago, and desperately wanted more.

His eyes burned into me as he owned the stage. Every time he glanced my way, which was often, I found myself pinned in place, my legs turned to jelly by the blaze of raw lust burning in his eyes.

Why is he looking at ME like that? I wondered. There were dozens of other women in the bar, prettier, richer, skinnier women half my size. Just about every woman in the bar was oozing desire for Chase, lining up around the stage area, all of them wearing sexy little outfits sized in the single digits instead of double.

Yet Chase had eyes only for me, with my size-eighteen mini skirt and three-inch heels elevating me to nearly six feet tall. I knew I looked good, for me, but compared to all these other model-looking women, I knew I shouldn't have a chance in hell with a guy like Chase. But yet here he came, burly arms swinging, eyes fixed on me like he was a lion stalking a gazelle across the savannah. I was no gazelle, but he didn't seem to care.

"You've got a great selection," Chase said, his voice rolling over me.

I was flustered enough to drop the CD I was holding. He was mere inches from me, gazing down at me with what could not possibly be, could never be, surely wasn't desire.

"Selection?" I asked.

Am I popping out of my top? I looked down at my chest, suddenly unable to put two thoughts together.

Chase laughed, a low, amused chuckle. "Your song selection. You have a lot of songs to choose from."

I glanced back up to meet Chase's eyes, and as our gazes met, Chase let his slide down to my cleavage and hung there, an obvious, intentional ogle.

"Oh," I muttered. "Yeah...well, can't be a DJ without music."

"True. But your selection is especially...vast." He was talking about my tits now.

"You sounded great," I said, because it was true, and a complete sentence.

"Thanks." He reached past me, his arm going over my shoulder and brushing my face, his lips now mere inches from mine as the whole bar watched.

I thought he was going to kiss me, but he grabbed a song request slip from the waist-high counter running along the wall behind me. He took a mini-pencil and scribbled something on the slip, and then handed it to me.

"Sing with me," he said. It wasn't quite a direct command, but almost.

I was tempted to say no, just to show him he couldn't order me around, but damn it, I wanted to sing with him. I was sure, in the same way I knew when I was nailing a song just right, Chase and I would sound incredible together. My deep alto voice would provide a perfect counterpoint to his powerful tenor.

We would make beautiful music together, I thought. I had to suppress a naughty giggle, because the thought had nothing at all to do with singing.

"I would love to," I said as I took the slip from his fingers.

Our fingers touched when I grabbed it from him, and I felt again an electric current zapping through my entire body from that one split-second contact.

If I felt such electricity from just our fingers touching, then dear god, what would it feel like to have his hands on my tits? Pinching my nipples and slipping his fingers into my...?

I actually, literally gasped as I forced the thought from my mind. Chase was still gazing at me, and now the gleam of lust was bearing down on me full force, unmistakable and undeniable and focused on me.

"Stop looking at me like that," I said.

"Like what?" His voice was pitched low so only I could hear, even though with the fill music

pounding from the speakers he could have spoken
in a yell and no one would have heard. He spoke
low on purpose, so I'd have to get closer to him.

It worked, and I wasn't protesting.

"Like you want me."

His eyes sparked and flashed, and the corners
of his luscious mouth tipped up in a smirk. "Oh,
but I do."

"You can't," I said.

"Why not?"

"Because I'm...?" I started, and then had to cut
myself off and grab for the mic, because the fill
song had ended and the next number was up and
needed introducing.

I read the name and song title, my brain working on autopilot. Chase was still standing there, his
brow furrowed in a frown. When I sat back down,
he moved to rejoin me, but had to step aside for a
line of people making song requests. I had to push
him from my mind after that, busy with sorting
CDs and prompter tracks and announcing songs,
and by the time I looked out at the crowd again,
he was gone.

I took my break at midnight, slipping outside
to the deserted alley behind the bar with a bottle of
beer. This was my quiet time, my five or ten minutes away from the crush of the crowd to gather
my thoughts and let my nerves settle. It was a dark,
narrow alley, lit by a single light hanging from a

string between adjacent buildings, shedding sickly orange light and long shadows. I leaned a shoulder against the rough brick of the bar's exterior wall and sipped my beer.

Chase's voice came from behind me. "You never put our song in the lineup."

I squealed, whirling around with my fist flying. The Dive was in an area where it didn't pay to let your guard down. I'm not a small girl, and I know how to punch. I've flattened men before, with my fists and with pool sticks and with beer bottles. I've knocked teeth loose and caused concussions. I'm not a brawler, but I can take care of myself against most men.

Chase caught my fist easily. He held my closed fist in his for a moment, then curled his fingers around my wrist and pulled me to him.

His other hand drifted up as he slowly and inexorably dragged me against his chest.

I flinched away from him, trying to get away from his hand, which I was sure held a knife, but then I realized it was empty and merely reaching for my face. The backs of his fingers brushed my cheek, and then he wrapped his hand around the nape of my neck and pulled my lips against his.

His kiss made my knees buckle. He was still holding my wrist up near our faces, as if worried I might haul off and hit him for kissing me. I thought about it. I really did. This guy was trouble. He just

wanted me because he thought I'd be easy, and desperate. A lot of guys assumed that, and a lot of
guys had gotten a rude awakening.

But Chase, the way he was kissing me…it didn't
feel like a guy who assumed he'd be in my pants.
He was kissing me like he hoped he'd be in my
pants, like he was working to get there, and I really
liked how it felt.

His fingers loosened on my wrists, and I tugged
my hand free. I didn't hit him. I let my arm drape
across his shoulders, and my fingers tangled in the
soft, dark hair on his neck.

He groaned, a low, animal sound in the very
bottom of his throat, a primal growl that had my
belly trembling. I wanted to hear that sound again,
wanted to feel the power of his voice and know
that I'd caused it. So, naturally, I grabbed his ass.

Oh, my sweet Lord. The man's ass was a perfect globe of muscle, and I swear it was made to
fit in my hands. Once I had a hold on that fine
piece of leather-cupped flesh, I couldn't let go. I
was actually factually electrified as if I'd grabbed a
high-voltage wire.

His chuckle was the same leonine rumble of
pleasure, but laced with amusement. He slipped his
hand from my neck and let it trace a sensuous, teasing line down my back to rest just above the swell
of my hip, no more sexual a touch than if we were
dancing in a club. I curved my spine into his palm.

Our kiss broke for a moment, and he pulled his face back to meet my eyes. His hands slipped down to grasp my buttocks, watching my reaction. I pressed into him, lifted up on my toes so he could get a better grip on me.

He kissed me again, and this time it wasn't a kiss meant to surprise, like the first two, quick and hard and shocking, all lips and startling power and zero finesse. This time, he kissed me slowly, languorous and deliberate and skillful. He let our lips meet, and then he slipped his tongue out to touch my teeth and explore the contours of my mouth, the corner where my upper and lower lips met, the hollow beneath my tongue, and then farther in to slide along the surface of my tongue.

I moaned then, a soft murmur of my vocal chords. Chase tugged my hips flush against his, and I felt a hard length between us. It was only a bulge against the leather of his pants, but it was enough to get me wetter than a rainforest between my legs.

My hands circled around away from his ass to slip between us, reaching to unbutton his pants. Even through his pants I could tell the man was endowed like a god.

"Just a taste." The words actually came out of my mouth.

"You can have more than a taste, sweetness," Chase said.

I didn't think he realized I was talking about his cock.

"I didn't mean your lips," I said.

What the hell is wrong with me? My brain seemed to be disconnected from the rest of me.

Chase pulled away long enough to meet my eyes. "I know," was all he said, giving me the smirk, that stupid, knowing quirk of his lips.

I wanted to wipe it off his face, either with my fist or my lips. I wasn't sure which. He was touching me and kissing me like he owned me, and it infuriated me and intoxicated me at the same time.

Intoxication had the upper hand, by far.

My hand found his stomach, and rested there as I warred with myself over whether or not I could bring myself to touch him farther down. I wanted to, of course I did, but I wasn't that kind of girl. I just wasn't. I was the girl that let guys convince her into bed. I didn't pursue them, because that never went well.

But Chase was pursuing me, wasn't he? That was the argument the horny side of me offered up. It was starting to sound like the logical side of me, too, which was odd. Usually the horny side and the logical side were telling me exact opposite things. So when they started agreeing with each other, I listened.

I sneaked my fingers underneath his shirt to touch his stomach, and the slab of muscle my hands found was ribbed and cut into deliciously soft yet hard divots and squares. It was a tempting playground, and normally I'd jump at the opportunity to rub my hands on Chase's abs, but right then I was in search of another, more dangerous place to explore.

The leather was rough and pebbled under my fingers as I dragged my hand south from his stomach to the waistband of his pants. The bulge was growing larger as my hands neared it, and I felt a tremble in his hands on my hips, the merest leaf-shake of his fingers, but it was enough. He wanted it, too. I mean, of course he did. He's a guy. All guys want their cocks touched.

But this was different, right? He wanted me to touch him. And it was right there, waiting for me. Sure, I didn't even know his last name, but here was this ridiculously gorgeous guy decked out in leather pants with a ripped body and what promised to be a deliciously enormous package, and he was all but claiming me as his, if only for tonight.

I found the button and slipped it through to let the tight pants spread apart, and then drew the zipper down, forcing myself to go slow, because you can't rush beauty. Then there was a thin layer of stretchy cotton between my hands and his cock, just black DKNY boxer-briefs that didn't stand a chance against my daring fingers. The bulge sprang free, and I pulled the band of the boxers away from his belly to get a glimpse of the glory contained therein.

Fuck me sideways! The man is hung like a porn star! It was too good to be true, surely. He would let me get a glimpse, maybe let me suck him off, which I would gladly do right there and then, but that would be it. No way he'd take me back to his place and fuck me proper.

Determined not to let such a golden opportunity go to waste, I touched him with my forefinger, just one reverent brush of the pad of my finger along the pre-come-glistening tip. He gasped, sucked in his belly, and throbbed his hips into my hand.

Oh, oh, oh my god.

Touching his cock was like eating chips; I couldn't stop after just one. I had to have more, had to get both hands around him, and yes, he was a two-hand man. Maybe even two and half, because for a big girl I have small hands. I wrapped my fingers around his girth and shoved his boxers farther down with the heel of my hand so I could fit my other palm around him.

He sucked in his breath and arched his back. "God, Anna. You're driving me crazy."

"I like hearing you say my name." I didn't mean to say that, but it slipped out, and Chase didn't seem to mind.

"Anna," he gasped.

I smeared his pre-come on his cock with a

hand-over-hand motion, and he writhed into my grip. He was nearly there, about to explode on my hands, and I wasn't about to stop. He put his hands on my ribcage, just beneath my breasts.

"Yes," I whispered, "touch my tits."

I felt the veins of his shaft pulsing under my touch. I dug one of my hands into his pants and cupped his heavy, tight testicles as I continued to work his length with the other hand. He was bucking up and down with his entire body, bending his knees and thrusting up with his entire torso, driving his cock through my slippery grip. His eyes were hooded and his breathing was coming in desperate gasps.

I was determined to make sure he damn well never forgot this experience, even if it was all we'd ever have together. I didn't care about getting off myself, momentarily; I knew I could go home and break out Mr. Pinky McVibrator and use this memory to come at least once, if not twice. I was multi-orgasmic, if only with myself. No guy had ever made me come more than once, and most never did at all.

"Anna, wait," Chase gasped, trying to back away. "This wasn't...I wanted to...with you?"

I didn't let him get away. He curled in over his stomach and clenched his muscles; I knew it was time. I dropped to my knees, wrapped my lips around his head, and sucked for all I was worth.

He couldn't speak, couldn't move, couldn't do anything but thrust his cock into my mouth and shoot his load into me. He shot, and he shot, and he shot, and I took it all, tasting the smoky, salty thickness against my tongue and my throat and for once not minding at all, for once actually understanding those girls who claim to love giving head.

I'll do it, every once in a while, just to make the guy feel good and to remind him who had the power, but I'd never enjoyed it before. I didn't dislike it, I just wasn't a "hooray, I'm sucking cock" kind of girl.

But Chase...oh, he came beautifully. He stretched his mouth wide and arched his back, fluttering his lovely, pulsing cock into me, holding back, restraining himself from cramming himself down the back of my throat.

When I'd milked him of every last drop, I tucked him back into his DKNY boxers, zipped up his pants, and buttoned him up.

"You have a beautiful cock," I told him, rising to my feet, "and you taste good, too."

I kissed him once, a fast, hard crush of the lips.

"Thanks for a good time, Chase," I said.

And with that I turned and made my exit.

"Wait," Chase growled, grabbing my arm. "You can't just leave. That wasn't what I...?"

I kept moving, despite his grip on my arm. "I have to finish my set."

He grabbed my other arm then, and pulled me forcefully back around to face him.

"I wasn't done with you yet."

I yanked my arm free, starting to be angry that he'd ruined my exit, and was in the process of ruining my memory of him. "Let go, Chase. You got what you wanted, didn't you? I've got to go back to work."

Chase's eyes narrowed and his brows furrowed. "I didn't ask you to do that."

I gritted my teeth. "Yeah, I know. You didn't ask for it, not in so many words, but guys like you know how to get what you want without asking for it. Especially from girls like me."

"Guys like me." Chase frowned and squeezed my arm hard enough to make me wince.

"Yeah. Guys like you. Talented, gorgeous guys who can get anyone they want."

"How do you know what I want? And what do you mean by 'girls like you'?"

I absolutely refused to answer that question. Storming out of the alley toward the front door, I rounded the corner just as my partner Jeff came looking for me. I haven't mentioned my partner yet, have I? Jeff...a stable, steady guy, a good business partner, better-than-average-looking, and a great singer. We DJed together, splitting the profits and making quite a bundle. We'd never been more than friends and partners, even though I knew he had a crush on me.

"Everyone's waiting, Anna," Jeff said. He knew me well enough to see I was upset. "Is everything okay?"

I was glad he hadn't come around the corner twenty seconds earlier; he wouldn't have done or said anything, but it would have hurt him to see me doing that to Chase, and I didn't want to lose a good partner.

"I'm fine, Jeff. Don't worry about it." I turned him by the shoulders and pushed him back through the front door of The Dive.

"Anna, wait." I felt Chase's hand on my arm. I spun around with my fist flying.

Of course, he caught it like he had the first time. Thank god Jeff was already inside, so he didn't see anything.

"Chase, seriously. We both know the score here."

"There's no score. Don't be like this. What you did felt great, better than great, but that wasn't what I was going for. I don't know why you're getting so upset all of a sudden. I like you, I want...?"

"Anna, let's go!" Jeff stuck his head out the door, saw me stumble as Chase told me he liked me.

"Hey, listen, buddy, I don't know what your game is, but Anna's not interested." Jeff thrust his chest out and strutted toward Chase, thinking he was defending me. Jeff was sweet, meant well, and was obviously fearless, since Chase was several inches taller and several pounds of muscle heavier.

I pushed Jeff back inside. "It's fine, Jeff. He's not bothering me. He was just leaving."

Chase's face darkened. "No, I wasn't." He strode past me, ignoring Jeff completely. "You owe me a song at least."

Jeff raised an eyebrow at me, and I shrugged, stifling a sigh.

We sang "Broken" by Seether and Amy Lee. I couldn't hold on to my conflicted feelings, not with Chase's dulcet growl braiding perfectly with my voice. The bar was silent as we sang, even the bartenders going still to watch. Tension rippled in palpable waves between Chase and me, propelling our performance into overdrive.

Sometimes while performing time itself seems to stop when you hit your notes just right. The music glides between the pores of your skin to bubble through your veins in place of blood, and you can't help but clutch the mic with both trembling hands and let the song flow out of you like blood from a wound. In those moments, when the music has replaced everything and even awareness of your own body has faded, you can't breathe, can't do anything but let the song own you, let the performance rocket through you. There's no people, no problems in your life, no buzz of alcohol in your blood or pain in your heart. Sharing that moment with another person...it's more intimate than sex. You and the other person lock eyes, bend at the waist to belt the notes into the mic, and invisible sun-hot flames burn between you, linking you. You could be the only two souls alive in the world.

When the song ended, I was exhausted, feeling as wrung out as if Chase and I had just gone three rounds in bed. The tension was thick enough to cut with a knife, and neither of us knew how to approach it. The chemistry required to share a song like Chase and I just had, that was rare. You could harmonize perfectly with someone, and even give great performances together like Jeff and I did every week, but to be able to join your souls together for the length of a song, and interpret the music and lyrics to have deeply personal meaning...you just didn't come across that every day.

The next several numbers felt flat, even to me. The rest of the bar seemed to feel it, reluctant to take the stage and sing, not when the memory of Chase's and my song still rang loud in the small space.

Eventually, a chant began. "Sing, Sing, Sing...."

The whole bar caught on, until the chant was echoing off the ceiling and the patrons pushed Chase and me onto the stage.

Jeff, ever the professional, stuck in a CD and sat back in the shadows.

When the first notes pounded from the speakers,

Chase and I rolled our eyes and sighed in tandem. Jeff had put on "I'd Do Anything For Love (But I Won't Do That)" by Meatloaf.

We killed it. No one could breathe, and I think I saw a few teary eyes as Chase and I sang, the roiling emotions between us ratcheting up even further with every note. I hated Jeff for putting on this song. I was trying SO hard not get attached, not to let my emotions lead me to a broken heart, which I knew was all that waited for me on the other side of anything with Chase.

The crowd went wild when the last note faded. We held hands and bowed, as if we were on stage at Harpos.

Jeff put on fill music and I vanished out the side door. Chase followed, of course.

"Chase, I can't…"

"Come home with me."

We spoke at the same time, and I was so shocked by his words that I could only stop, stunned. Then he kissed me. You know how in *The Princess Bride* it says in the history of the world there's only been five truly great kisses? Well, this one blew them all away. Yes, I know that's the next line from the movie, but I've never thought the kiss between Westley and Buttercup was all that great, for one thing, and for another, this kiss between Chase and me…the stars froze in the sky, and the moon went dark, and all the world stopped and stared, awed at the sheer, breathtaking passion blazing between us.

At least, that's how it felt to me.

When we broke apart, Chase pulled a business card from his back pocket that already had his address scribbled on it in neat, blocky capital letters. No phone number or email address, just his physical house address.

"I'm going home," Chase said. "If you'd like to know what I want to do with you, come over after your set. If you don't show up, you'll never see or hear from me again. It's up to you."

I took the card in trembling fingers. "Chase...I—"

He kissed me again to cut me off. "It's up to you, Anna. If you're too afraid, I'll understand. Just remember, you never know what's possible until you risk finding out."

And then he was gone, roaring away on a sleek black Ducati motorcycle.

I stood on the sidewalk in front of Chase's house. It was a modest one-story ranch-style home, a square of grass in front, a detached garage, cracked driveway, and a tasteful lamppost in front. The front porch light was on, despite the fact that it was past three in the morning.

I forced my feet to leave the sidewalk and take the steps up to the front door. My finger hesitated on the doorbell, and then, with closed eyes and a hammering heart, I pushed it.

Chase was at the door within seconds, still in his leather pants but without his shirt.

Holy hell. I'd felt the muscles of his stomach, had seen his biceps, but nothing could prepare me for the sight that greeted me through the storm door. Pure male perfection, cut muscles defined with artistic clarity, dusky skin taut and hairless, inked across the pectorals and biceps with a stunning full-color red dragon wrapping entirely around his torso, writhing with every breath, every shifting of his muscles.

I froze, unable to tear my eyes away. Chase opened the door, took me by the hand, and pulled me in. He'd meant for me to move past him, but I landed pressed against his hot skin and bulky muscles, hands slipping and sliding across his broad shoulders and ridged back, around to his sides and then his chest.

"Why am I here?" I breathed.

Chase grinned down at me. "Can't you guess?" He pulled me into the house, closing the front door with his foot.

I shook my head. "Nope. I'm a terrible guesser." I pressed my lips to his shoulder blade, and then his neck. "Are we here for pretzels? I am a little drunk."

"You don't seem drunk," Chase said. His hands were resting on my hips, letting me kiss his skin.

"Not drunk, then. Tipsy. Enough to wonder if this is real."

"It's real." He dragged his fingers through my hair, wrapping his fist into it near the nape of my neck.

He tilted my head backward so I was looking up at him, lips parted in anticipation of his kiss.

"I must be dreaming," I said.

He kissed me, and it wasn't quite the kiss he'd given me in the parking lot a few hours ago, but it was close.

"Your lips don't feel like a dream." He ran his strong hands across my mini-skirted backside. "Your ass doesn't feel like a dream. It feels real enough to me."

"Are you sure? There's an awful lot of fabric in the way," I said.

"True. We should fix that." Chase's fingers explored the skirt until he found the zipper, tugged it down, slipped his hands between the skirt and my skin to push it down.

His hands on my bare skin felt like tongues of fire along my flesh. I couldn't keep a moan from escaping my lips. Chase buried his nose against my neck at the sound, digging his fingers into the flesh of my ass. I was wearing a thong, a bit of blue fabric across my vag with a few strings around my hips and down my ass crack. He traced the line of the strings, dipping down between the globes of my butt to cup each cheek, then up to my stomach.

"Lift your arms up," he said.

I complied without thinking. He was commanding me, and I normally hated being ordered around, but the gentle promise in his voice had me raising my hands over my head. He drew my shirt off, leaving me standing in the middle of his living room clad in only a matching bra and panties. Chase stepped back away from me.

"God, you're beautiful," he said.

"Okay, sure. Shut up and kiss me again."

"I want to look at you first." Chase stopped just out of arm's reach. "You're a goddess."

I rolled my eyes. "Yeah, right." I planted my hand on my hip and put my weight on one leg, posing for him even as my mouth betrayed me.

Chase went from gazing appreciatively to gripping my arms in anger within the space of an eyeblink. "You're beautiful. You're perfect. I wouldn't change a thing about you."

"You're hurting my arms," I said. "You're sweet, but I'm a bit self-conscious about my size."

Chase loosened his grip, but didn't let go. His eyes bored into mine. "Never, ever say that about yourself again, Anna. You. Are. Beautiful." He stepped into me, and now his skin was brushing against mine, the leather of his pants rough against my legs, his bulge hard and thick against my stomach.

He took me by the hands and led me down a short, narrow hallway to the master bedroom, a simple, tasteful space, light and airy and masculine, neat and smelling of candles.

He'd lit candles. The man had lit candles. A dozen of them on his dresser and on the trunk at the foot of his bed. I melted.

"Why are you doing this for me?" The words were choked from my lips.

Chase kept pulling me towards the wide bed, covered with a simple comforter and a few pillows. "Because I like you. Because I want you. Because you deserve it."

"No, I don't. Not with you."

"Why not?" He stopped pulling and stood holding my hands.

I couldn't meet his gaze, kept my head down and stared at his bare feet. "Because I'm…" I drew a deep breath and forced the words past quivering lips. "Because I'm…a big girl."

Chase's fingers clenched mine, and his eyes went from fiery with lust to wavering with sudden understanding and something awfully like compassion.

"Big?" His voice was incredulous. "You think I couldn't want this with you, just because you're not a size zero? Unbelievable."

He kissed my shoulder, the right one, on the round curve where my arm began.

"You're perfect the way you are, Anna. You're a work of art." He kissed my chest, just above my left breast. "Don't ever, ever change. Don't ever let anyone tell you you're anything less than a glorious, beautiful sex goddess. Look at me, Anna." His voice was gentle, but firm. He touched my chin and forced me to obey. His eyes were burning with the fiery lust once more. "Listen to me."

"No. Just shut up and fuck me already." I looked away, watched a candle flicker.

"I don't want to fuck you, Anna. I mean, I do, but I want more to do so much more than that."

"Don't mess with me, Chase. This is supposed to be easy. I know what this is. It's sex. One night of hot monkey sex, and then you go back to your life with a sexy little skinny bitch who you get it on with in all sorts of hot positions I could never do."

"You don't know shit, if that's what you think."

The tone in his voice pulled my eyes up to his once more.

"I don't even know your last name," I said.

"Delany." He unhooked my bra with one dexterous hand.

He brushed the shoulder straps off and the bra fell into his waiting hand. He set it aside and gazed at my breasts.

"Chase Delany," I whispered, as he leaned in toward me.

"That's me. And what's your last name, sweet-ness?" He put his lips on my chest, an inch beneath my throat, and I instinctively arched into his hot, wet mouth.

"Devine."

He stopped at looked up at me. "Seriously? Your name is Anna Devine?" His mouth returned to my flesh, and this time his lips found the rising mound of my breast. "You really are a sex god-dess, then, Anna Devine."

"I'm not. I'm—"

He straightened, and his gaze nearly knocked me over in its intensity. "Say it." He took one of my tits in his hand, hefting the significant weight of my thirty-eight triple-D breast, then the other, running the pad of his thumb across my taut nipples. "Say it, Anna Devine. Say, 'I'm a sex goddess.'"

I met his gaze, steady and hard, and pressed my lips together.

His eyes twinkled. "You'll say it. You'll say it before I'm through with you."

He knelt down in front of me, staring up at me through the mountains of my breasts, his hands around my waist to rest on the swell of my ass. His fingers curled through the strings of my thong and he drew it down over my hips, dragging it slowly, never taking his eyes off me.

Oh, lord, I thought, as he brought the panties

down past my knees. *He is not...no...he can't be serious...oh, sweet Jesus, he is.*

His tongue ran up my inner thigh to the hollow where my hip met my leg. My muscles twitched and my breath caught. He kissed my belly, low, just above the mound of my pussy. He was still gazing up at me, even as his tongue dipped down to run up the other side of my thigh, brushing just past my labia once more.

"What are you doing?" I put my hands in his hair, meaning to tug him up.

"Worshipping a goddess."

He smiled at me, then pushed at my thigh with gentle, insistent fingers. My stance widened on its own, my legs spreading apart to give him access.

His nimble, probing, licking tongue swiped up between my lower lips, a wet heat against my most sensitive area. I couldn't even gasp then. He pressed his mouth to my opening and his tongue flicked in, darting against my clit, a single tender brush, but it was enough to make my legs buckle. His arms went back up and circled my waist, supporting me. I put my hands on his thick shoulders and threw my head back as his tongue went back in, and this time stayed in. He licked in slow, lazy, wide circles around the cluster of nerves, sending shockwaves through my body. I moaned. I couldn't help it, not with his tongue drawing from my trembling loins an ecstasy I'd never known existed.

The slow circles tightened and sped up, and the shockwaves narrowed in waveform, rolling over me until I was dipping my knees at each pulse of his tongue against my flesh, pressing my mound against his rough stubble, his powerful arms supporting me.

I cried out, a rasping whimper, and went limp. He caught me, lifted me, actually factually lifted me clear off the ground and onto the bed before I could catch my breath. And then, before the world stopped spinning, he was holding my legs apart, resting my knees on his shoulders and spearing his tongue into me once more, relentless, merciless.

I was on the verge of blowing apart in his hands when he abruptly stopped, disappeared. I made a mewling noise in protestation.

"Will you trust me?" Chase's voice came from above me.

I fluttered my eyes open to see Chase holding a necktie in each hand. I knew what he was planning, and I was torn between terror and excitement.

He seemed to understand my hesitation. "If you start to panic for real, just say, 'Chase, please stop.' Three words, and I'll untie you immediately."

I nodded and held my hands out to him. Chase grinned, a wicked smile of anticipation. He tossed the ties on the pillow at the head of the bed, took my hips in his hands, and flipped me over to my stomach. I gasped, shocked. He had tossed me like I was nothing, and it had simultaneously made my heart pitter patter in awe, and made my pussy go wet all over again. I was still feeling waves of pleasure from his earlier attentions, and now, with one movement, I was anticipating more.

He took my hands in one of his and tugged me forward so I was forced to crawl with him to the headboard. He took one of my hands and used the necktie to bind my wrist to the post. I tugged on it, but couldn't pull it loose. He did the same to the other hand, and now I was captive for him, hands bound in front of me.

"Put your knees underneath you," he said. I did as he told me. "Spread them apart. Let me see all of you."

My heart was hammering in my chest, but I did as he instructed, spreading my knees as far apart as they would go, lowering my chest to the bed so my nether regions were exposed to him. Chase rumbled in his chest, a noise of appreciation that made me tremble and gush even wetter. I felt his weight press the bed down, and then I felt a warm, calloused palm brush across my backside, caressing and then probing toward my core, finding my pussy with two fingers and stroking the lips, only brushing them at first. I let out my breath in a gasp and tried to twist around to look at him, but he stilled me with a hand on my spine.

"Don't look. Close your eyes and let me touch you," Chase said, and he pressed a finger to my clit, stifling any words I might have said.

I closed my eyes and laid my forehead on the blanket beneath me, losing myself in sensation. I had been so close to coming not long ago, and now, with a few strokes of his fingers I was there again.

I felt him lie down and his hair tickled me; just as I wondered what he was doing, I felt his tongue hit me again. He lay underneath me with his mouth pressed against my pussy, breathing into me, hot air blowing against me and eliciting a long gasp. Then his tongue licked upward into me, found my clit and swirled it, circled around it, pushed against it, and now the explosions began once more, rocketing through me. I moved into him, rocking my body into the growing orgasm.

The shockwaves were so close together now they were indecipherable from each other, a single cresting, crashing tidal wave. The tsunami broke and I came with a shriek, my inner muscles clenching as pure, sinful pleasure washed through me in a flood.

He didn't relent with my cry, though. He kept licking and spearing, putting two fingers inside me and curling up to find my G-spot. Light exploded behind my eyes as explosions continued to rock my body, one after another, a thrilling detonation for every swipe of his tongue against my damp nub, a billowing concussion for every caress of his fingers against the rough patch of skin deep inside my walls.

I curled in, knees tight, fingers gripping the ties with white knuckles as I came and came and came, and still he didn't give in. I had to beg him to stop so I could catch my breath, so I could let my muscles release.

"I've...I've never had so many orgasms... before," I said, collapsed face down on the bed.

"You haven't even started to come for me," Chase said.

"No, I mean I've never had so many orgasms before, ever. Combined, in all my life." I arched my back as he caressed my spine. "At least, not that weren't self-induced."

"Then we'll have to make sure you lose count," he said.

I craned my neck over my shoulder. "I want to see you," I said. "Let me touch you."

"I'm not ready for that yet."

"Just one hand? So I can feel you? Please." I didn't mind begging.

Chase slipped off the bed and moved around to the headboard. He untied one of my hands and stood beside me, just within reach. I ran my hand down his torso, marveling at the cords and ridges of muscle. I'd found my breath, and now my own lust was boiling over. I wanted to feel him, needed to see him nude before me. I'd seen him earlier, but that was with his pants still on. I needed them off, so I could see him in all his glory.

The button and zipper were undone in a single jerking motion. I tugged the pants down. They were tight and didn't want to cooperate, especially with one hand, but I got them off and he was standing in front of me, a tiny bit of black fabric stretched tight across his waist. He was huge in his boxers, and I licked my lips at the memory of him in my mouth.

Just another taste.

"You can taste me all you want," Chase said, and I realized I'd spoken aloud.

I dug underneath the elastic to touch his hip, pushed the boxers down, and gripped his muscular ass with my one free hand. The waistband caught on his engorged tip, and I pulled the fabric away from his cock to get them down around his thighs. His shaft was standing at attention, bobbing against his stomach as he breathed. He was naked then, and I could only stare.

"God, you are so gorgeous," I said.

Eight-pack abs, broad pectoral muscles and thick arms, a perfect V leading down to his cock, which was, in a word, perfect. His legs were like tree trunks, his ass a wonderland of muscle and flesh, his hair a sweep of black inky strands, his face a symmetrical sculpture of angles and planes, hard and masculine. And his eyes, deep, dark brown, almost black, glittering orbs of expression.

I took in his beauty, drinking him in as if I couldn't ever get enough. But, inevitably, my gaze was drawn back to his cock, which was just begging to be touched, held, kissed. I reached for him, let myself explore his length with my fingers and palm.

He closed his eyes as I touched him, moving his hips in imperceptible rolls. I watched as the hole at the tip began to leak clear fluid under my ministrations.

He tried to pull away. "I can't take it, not without exploding all over you."

"What if I want you to?" I drew him closer by his cock. "What if I want you to come all over me? Is that what you want? To come on my face? On my tits?"

I moved my hand on him in an increasing rhythm as his hips began to buck. His eyes flew open, and he stepped away.

"No." He forced my hands away from his throbbing cock. "I don't want that. Not yet, anyway. I want to be inside you."

He re-tied my hand to the bedpost, climbed onto the bed behind me, and took my hips in his hands, his heat radiating into my skin, our bodies pressed together in a delicious point of contact at my bottom. He was poised to spear into me, but he hesitated once more.

"Chase, please," I heard myself say. I wanted him inside me. I didn't care if I had to beg to get it.

"First things first." He leaned over to the bed-side table and opened a drawer, pulled out a string of condoms, and ripped one free.

"I'm on the pill and I'm clean."

He froze. "I'm clean, too, but even the pill isn't—"

"I'm not worried," I said. He still hesitated. "Just take me. Please."

He leaned over me, his hard length pressed along the crease of my buttocks. He reached around my body to caress my breasts with both hands, his palms brushing my nipples, sending lightning thrills through me. Still on my knees, I hunched my back and rocked my hips backward into his.

He settled back on his knees, probed the entrance of my pussy with one hand, and guided himself in with other, finally giving me what I so badly wanted: his incredible god-cock, deep inside me, his strokes slow and gentle and careful.

"Oh...my...god..." I breathed, as he drew out, fluttered at my entrance, and then plunged back in. "Chase...don't stop, please."

"Never, never," he said, his words rhythmed to the crush of his shaft into me. "God, you feel so good, so goddamned perfect."

He plunged deep inside me, ground his hips against my ass, leaning over me again. One of his hands pinched my nipple, rolled it between two fingers, the other on my hip, encouraging me into him.

His thrusts were deliberately measured, mere pulsations of hips against mine as if he too was fighting for control. I didn't want control. I didn't want him to be able to keep the rhythmic pace he was setting. I wanted to make him wild, to make him break loose with insanity.

I abandoned all pretense." Don't hold back," I told him. "I'm not delicate. You won't break me."

He responded with fingers diving down to find my clitoris and drive me even wilder. The explosions began in my belly, spread to my lungs and my toes, and then to my inner muscles, and last to my brain. The intensity of this orgasm, with him flush against me, muscles surrounding me in walls of strength and heat and man, with Chase gasping in my ear, whispering my name...it put all other sensations in my life to shame.

I saw the heavens, felt pure ecstasy, unadulterated glory. I whimpered as the climax began, and then, when he kept pushing into me, the whimpers turned to moans, and the moans to sobs, and then, at the full, furious apex of wonder and joy bursting through my body and soul, I screamed.

He wasn't done yet.

He untied me. I moved to lie down on my back, but Chase only shook his head. I remained on my hands and knees, waiting for him to tell me what he wanted.

He lay down on his back. "Ride me, Anna."

I shook my head. He pinched a nipple between his fingers and tugged me toward him until the twinge of pain had me moving astride him, settling my weight on him gradually.

I let myself sit there for a moment, but then he moved his hips and I tried to move off him. He held me in place.

"Chase, no, let me down. I could hurt you."

He just grinned and lifted me up by my hips and impaled me onto him, thrusting deep, silencing my gasps as he began to push me back up the peak toward climax once more, and I couldn't help but move my hips to match him.

"I'm not delicate," he said. "You won't break me."

"Yes, I will," I said.

But I didn't move to get off him. I couldn't stop myself. I'd never been like this with a man. No one had ever been brave enough to try this with me, or strong enough. But Chase, oh, the man held me in place and rocked into me, and his grunting and gasping drove me wild. He lost control, his cock throbbing into me in wild pulses. His head tilted back and his eyes closed, his hands reaching for my tits again and fondling them and lifting them; he arched his back, and used the strength of his core to lift me off the bed with each thrust. I took him, all of him, swallowing his immense size with each downward crush of my hips onto him.

He opened his eyes and watched me, his lips curling in a wicked smile of satisfaction.

"Yes, yes," he groaned, driving into me with each syllable. "Just like this. God, god, oh, god, Anna, yes. Oh, I'm so close now."

I was at climax again, and I leaned forward, put my hands on his chest, and let my weight fall on his shoulders. Something deep inside me shifted then, as he supported me with just his body, holding me off the bed with his hips and his hands and his shoulders, coursing into me, wild and abandoned to the passion flaming between us.

I lost myself to him then. I drowned myself in the crashing ocean of pleasure.

He gripped my hips in bruising fingers to drag me down onto him harder and harder with each thrust of his cock.

Time slowed and stopped then, as I felt his muscles tense and clench around me, felt his cock tighten and release. He roared, a bellow of male pleasure, and I felt the hot jet of his seed wash through me, a pulse of liquid and a thrust, a growl, and then he rocked again, filling me with yet more seed, and now I was exploding on top of him, coming apart in his hands. I fell forward and our lips met as we climaxed together, my inner muscles clamping around his still-thrusting, still-coming shaft.

Then I completely and totally lost it, overcome by sheer orgasmic pleasure and by fear and wonder and abandonment. He was shuddering into me, all pretense of rhythm lost as he gasped ragged inbreaths, and long quaking out-breaths. His arms wrapped around my back and neck and clutched me to him.

"Say it," he breathed into my ear.

He was still shuddering, and I felt a thrill of power knowing I'd done that to him.

"I am a sex goddess." I said the words one syllable at a time, starting to feel it.

"Yes, yes...you are. You're my sex goddess." Chase kissed my throat and my shoulder and my chin and my forehead, holding me in his powerful arms.

"Tell me in two words who you are," he said. "Start there."

I shook my head, calming now, but still shuddering with sobs and aftershocks.

"Tell me," he said.

The words came unbidden. "Big. A singer."

He shook his head. "You're not big. You're perfect."

"I know what I am. I can't change it, and I'm fine with that."

"You're perfect the way you are. I made love to you as you are."

Goddamn it. I shook my head and a fat tear plopped onto his chest.

"What are you so afraid of? Why can't you believe what I'm saying? Not every guy in the world likes women to be stick figures. Not every guy in the world want his woman to be all skin and bones. I happen to like your softness and curves, just like I like your attitude and your style. I like the way you screamed when you came for me."

He pressed his mouth to my ear. The next words he spoke broke me.

"I made love to you, Anna Devine. I made love to a goddess." I scrambled off the bed, shaking my head at him. "I mean it, Anna. I mean every word."

He stretched out a hand, and I shrank away, but he touched me anyway, and the same electric spark shot through me as the first time our hands had touched.

He pulled me toward him until his broad chest was pillowing my face, and the soft thump-thump of his heartbeat was all I could hear.

I slept better than I had in all my life.

I woke the following afternoon to an empty bed and a house smelling like coffee and bacon and sex.

I found Chase sitting with a cup of coffee in one hand, his cell phone in the other, and a grim look on his face.

"What is it?" I asked. "What's wrong?"

"It's complicated," he said, getting up to make me a cup of coffee. "I just heard from my agent. My band is getting signed to a major record label."

I sat down next to him and sipped the coffee. "Then what's with the sad face?"

He set his phone down and covered my hand with his. "I have to be in New York by tomorrow afternoon. I'm not sure when, if ever, I'll be back."

Then I understood. He had to leave me. I nodded slowly.

"I get it." I scalded my mouth on the coffee.

"This was the phone call I've been waiting for my whole life," he said, staring at the phone as if it had betrayed him. "And up until a week ago, it would have been the best news of my life. Then I met you."

I squeezed his hand. "It still is the best news of your life. Don't let me...don't let some random girl you had sex with stop you from being happy about this. I'll be fine. I knew all along this would be a one-time thing."

He glared at me, eyes hard but wavering with emotion. "But I didn't. God, Anna, I wish you could see yourself like I see you. You're not just some random girl I had sex with."

I couldn't face the emotion in his voice, how fraught with tension he was. I gathered my clothes, dressed in the bathroom, and found my purse.

"Thanks for a great time, Chase. Congratulations, and good luck in New York." I didn't turn to look at him as I spoke.

I opened the door, pushed open the storm door and took a step out, and then his next words froze me solid.

"Come with me," he said.

The Long Drive Home

THE DRIVE HOME FROM CHASE'S HOUSE was the longest trip of my life. My roommate Jamie would have called it "the walk of shame."

The walk of shame is when you've got your panties in your purse, you're a little sore between your thighs but not quite sexually sated, and you have a walk from his door to your car in the predawn chill that seems several miles long. You can almost see your breath in the gray hazy light, even if it's July. Your car has dew on the windows and the seat is cold against your legs, and the steering wheel is hard and frozen against your palms. The engine rolls over sluggishly, and you don't want to turn on the heater because you know by the time it warms up you'll be almost home.

You don't turn on the radio, because you want to be alone with your thoughts. You might wish you'd been able to stay over a bit longer and get some real sleep, because you've got work later in the day and you know you won't be able to sleep now but you'll be a zombie later. You might be ashamed of yourself because he seemed so awesome and sexy in the bar, and even when you got back to his place. The sex might have been okay, or even pretty good, and you got off but it just didn't quite satisfy you on some indefinable but visceral level. And now you're on the way home at four or five in the morning and you have awful morning-after-the-bar breath and a queasy drank-too-much stomach.

You know you'll never see him again because you didn't offer your phone number and he didn't ask, which meant he just wanted a hook-up for the night. You might be pretending you wanted the same thing. You tell yourself as you drive just over the speed limit through the brightening yellow dawn that it's fine. It was fun, you had a good time, and that's all it was meant to be. But, deep down, you were hoping it would turn into something more. You hoped that maybe he'd wake up while you were getting dressed and offer you coffee. You'd hold the mug in both hands and discover that he's just as sexy as you remember, if not more so, and god, he's actually funny and charming, and coffee would turn into breakfast at

National Coney Island and an exchange of phone numbers and email addresses and suddenly he'd be your boyfriend.

Instead, you're alone in your car, he's asleep still, and you noticed as you stuffed your tits into your bra that he's got a snaggle tooth and his eyes are too far apart and his mouth is lopsided, and you sort of remember his cock not being all that big, and really, the orgasm was more of a low rumble than anything resembling fireworks. Of course, the morning after a hook-up, no one is attractive. You imagine, as you run that yellow light, that he'll wake up and flick on Sports Center and drink coffee and wonder if you were as hot he remembered. Of course, you won't be there ,so he'll have the luxury of relying solely on his memory rather than facts, whereas you got a good look at Mr. One Night Stand while he was sleeping and you *know* he wasn't as hot as when you were half-drunk.

This is what I was thinking as I drove home. Chase would still be sitting at his table, trying to reconcile his lifelong dream coming true with the fact that it meant he and I couldn't ever really be anything more than one night of hot sex.

Hot sex. God, that term bugs me. I mean, who thinks of sex in terms of anything other than hotness? If it's lukewarm sex, it's probably only happening once. If it's cold sex, then you're probably not even finishing.

So Chase and I didn't have hot sex. No, we had earth-shaking sex. *Universe*-altering sex. Life-changing sex.

There was the truth of it. That one night of heaven with Chase Delany had changed me. He'd wanted me. He'd wanted me despite the fact that I *was* "plus-size." Not just despite, but *because of*. I nearly cried right there in the car, remembering his eyes and his voice as he looked at me, as he touched me. He made me come harder than I'd ever thought a girl could come, and made me admit, out loud, that I was a sex goddess.

Cupcake goddess, maybe. Jaeger goddess, maybe. Sex goddess? Me? Psshh. Yeah, right.

Anna Devine is *not* a sex goddess. But I'd felt like one with Chase. I'd realized I could make him feel good. I could give him pleasure. He wanted what I had. He wanted *me*. Me. It came back to that one fact as I sat at a red light, wishing I had more coffee. He wanted to be with me, to have sex with me, to touch my body, to kiss my skin.

My experience with sex thus far in my life had not prepared me to feel that way. My first time wasn't fun. We'd been virgins and it had been awkward and uncomfortable and messy. It's kind of funny now, looking back, but it hadn't been then. He'd gone on to date the prom queen, and had never looked at me again after that night in Hazel Park in the back of his '91 Lincoln Continental. It was almost like he'd used me to get rid of his virginity, wasted it on the fat girl so he could get the real experience with a girl who was actually hot. That's what I'd felt afterward, and when I ran into him at a reunion five years later, I'd realized I was probably right. He'd turned into a local politician, and you know how *those* guys are.

After that, sex was something bestowed on me, seemingly more out of pity than anything else. Lie there with him above you, not looking at you. A little kissing to start off, then he grabs your tits and squeezes too hard, pinches your nipples too hard. He shoves his hand down your pants and gropes a few inches too low with clumsy fingers. Let him tear your clothes off, fumble with your bra strap, try not to shield your breasts with your arms as he climbs on and rams into you without so much of a courtesy lick, or at least lube. God knows you don't feel *prepared*, as it were, so it's dry as a desert down there, but he doesn't care. He's already coming and he just uses his own spooge to lube you up for a few more stuttering strokes, smearing you from back to front with all kinds of mess. Roll off, turn over, snore. You're left unsatisfied, frustrated, wanting an orgasm yourself, but your own fingers just aren't doing the trick and he's done for the night, so there you are, frustrated with no relief in sight.

Or you have guys who expect you to go down on them because you're the big, desperate girl, so *of course* you'd willingly and *gratefully* give him head, just for the gracious gift of getting to touch a man's actual flesh-and-blood cock rather than something rubber and battery-powered. Once upon a time, I had been that girl.

But when a guy tried to jab his cock through the back of my throat, and then hit me when I protested, I vowed to never ever act out of desperation again. A man would want me, or I wouldn't do a damn thing.

Which only made what had happened with Chase all the more confusing. Chase was a god among men. He was the kind of guy who gets out of limousines to the staccato lightning of flash-bulbs, the kind of guy who sets fashion trends and appears in *People* on a weekly basis. And he'd come after me. It felt surreal. The entire thing, the kiss in the Ram's Horn parking lot, the song at The Dive, the endless paradise of last night...it couldn't have been real.

I pinched myself hard enough to leave a mark, but the memories persisted in being real. My pussy insisted on being pleasantly sore. It was real. He was real. He'd wanted me.

No matter how many times I said it to myself, I couldn't believe it. He had to have an ulterior motive, right? Why else would he have brought me back to his house? He could have had anyone. He had only to beckon, and flocks of supermodels would come honking and squawking to his side, eager to please him. But instead, he'd wanted me. Anna Devine. DJ, plus-size, chronically lonely and under-sexed.

I'd given up on sex being something incredible, since it never lived up to the fuss everyone made out of it.

And then Chase happened, and I suddenly wasn't just a pretty-enough plus-size girl, or kind-of-hot for a big girl, and sex wasn't just "meh" anymore. I was beautiful and desirable, and sex was incredible.

I wanted to swing the car into a U-turn and race back to Chase's house, throw him down on the bed, or even the kitchen table, and ride him to climax again and again. I wanted to feel him above me. I wanted to taste him, touch him, feel the sweat bead on his skin and hear him groan as he came.

But I couldn't. He was leaving for New York, and he wasn't coming back. He'd invited me to go with him, but it had been a last-minute thing, impulsive, ridiculous. I couldn't actually just up and go to New York City on a whim with a guy I'd just met.

Sex with a guy I'd just met was one thing. A life-changing move across the country to a city where I knew no one was another thing entirely.

But god, he'd made me feel so good. Not just physically, but about myself. For one night, I knew what it felt like to be a woman wanted by a man. How could I let that go?

I made it home, sneaked past Jamie's half-closed door, and crawled in bed. I wouldn't sleep, I didn't think, but it felt so good to be in my own bed. It was freezing at first, the sheets cold from long hours of disuse, but after a few minutes they warmed up and I felt myself drowsing.

I fell asleep thinking of Chase. I fell asleep holding on to the feeling of being desired.

Big Girls Do It Wetter

GOD, I WAS SO CLOSE. I wanted it so bad. I was on the edge, just moments from making myself come, but...I couldn't. I'd tried, and tried, and tried. I lay on my bed, Mr. Pinky McVibrator in both hands, using all my tricks and all my best memories, but... nothing. I could get close, writhing on the bed, gasping and moaning and full of aching pressure between my thighs, but no matter what I did, I couldn't get myself past the edge into orgasm.

I had the vibrator turned to high, the humming audible in my silent bedroom, I had it plunging inside me, two fingers circling my aching, sensitive nub, and I had a firm image of Chase in my mind. In my fantasy, he was tied to a bed, hands and feet bound by his silky neckties, erection throbbing and dripping dew against his belly, just waiting for me to climb aboard and ride him like a prize bull.

I could almost feel him inside me, but…it didn't take me there. His hands weren't around my waist, urging me onward. His voice wasn't in my ear, whispering my name. He wasn't giving me gentle commands and wrapping his brawny arms around me.

He wasn't here, and I couldn't come without him.

It had been four days since I'd last orgasmed, and it was an eternity. Four days since I walked out of Chase's house, still aching between my thighs from the vigor of his lovemaking.

He watched me go, sadness in his eyes. He'd argued for a moment or two, but he realized I wasn't going to change my mind, and let me go.

I wanted to go with him. New York? Alone with Chase and his wonderful god-cock? Thanks, yes. But…he was going for his career. It was his big break. He didn't need me there, hanging on him, waiting for him to come back.

Besides, I'd known him for a week. One week. Two meetings. He'd kissed me the first day we met, and we'd slept together the second time.

Slept together. Such a trivial, meaningless phrase in the face of what really happened. Chase showed me what sex was like, what it could be, even for a big girl like me.

Big girl. I'd rolled that phrase around in my mind since he left. What did it mean, really? What did it signify? My clothes size? The number on the scale when I dared step on it? The shape of my body or the heft of my breasts and the swell of my backside?

No, what I realized was my use of the phrase "big girl" in reference to myself was nothing more than a self-categorization. I identified myself as that, so that's what I became.

Yeah, I know. Diets and exercise and eating right and it's not about what you eat but how much and why...blah blah blah. I'd tried it all. I could get to a certain point, and then my body stopped shrinking. It just held where it was and refused to change any more, until further efforts turned into bashing my head against the wall. So I kept myself at the point where I wouldn't lose any more weight and learned to accept it as the best I'd get.

But then I met Chase, and he thought I was beautiful. He didn't say it...well, he did, over and over again...but it was his actions that showed me he thought I was beautiful. It was in the way he touched me, in the way he kissed me and held me and made love to me. It was the fact that he considered it making love rather than having sex or fucking.

All this, from one night. Lordy lord. I was so mixed up, so completely screwed up in the head now, and it was all Chase's fault. I was addicted to his body, to being in bed with him, from one night.

I had a friend in high school who tried crack once at a party. She tried it once, got high on it once, one single time, and that was it. She was hooked. OD'd a few years later.

Well, Chase was my drug. Once, and I was hooked.

The problem was, he was gone, and I couldn't get him back. Not without chasing him across the country. Chasing Chase.

I tossed the sex toy across the room, not bothering to clean it first. There was no point.

DJing that night was hellish. I'd begged off my last shift the weekend Chase left. I went home, got drunk with my roommate, and stayed that way all day, marinating in my despair. Jaime never asked what was bothering me, because she's awesome that way. She knew I'd tell her when I wanted to, when I was ready.

I wasn't ready.

So now, with my first shift halfway through, I was a mess. I was cranky, bitchy, and off my game.

Jeff was setting up the speakers and mixer board while I sorted CDs and songbooks.

He was holding the speaker above his head with one hand and trying to spin the knob to tighten it in place, but it wouldn't catch for some reason, and he was getting frustrated. Those speakers are heavy, remember. Most people can't lift them above their head with one hand. Jeff's a beast like that. I watched him, grunting and sweating as he fiddled with the knob, his habitual long-sleeved T-shirt falling down around his forearms.

I suddenly realized how attractive Jeff really was. Maybe it was my raging libido or desperate need to get off, but right then, with his face contorted in irritation, his muscles bulging against the fabric of his shirt...he'd never been sexier to me.

Sure, I'd noticed in an off-hand way that he was attractive, but I'd never considered him before, and I suddenly wasn't sure why not.

"Anna, give me a hand, will you? This thing is stuck." Jeff's voice snapped me out of my rumination.

He put both hands to the speaker and held it while I got the knob to work. He was inches from me, the musk of male sweat in my nostrils, the heat of his body radiating into me. So close, yet so far.

I had a sudden, crazy desire to press my body into him, to see what his arms felt like around me. I was leaning, shifting my weight...and then he was gone. His eyes were on me, though, and I knew he'd felt it.

I shook my head. *What the hell am I thinking?* I couldn't afford distractions, not with Jeff. He was my partner, my business friend. Nothing else. It couldn't work.

Plus, he just wasn't Chase.

Yeah, but he's not far behind. My libido was piping up now, telling me what it wanted. And it wanted a taste of Jeff, a look at him without his long-sleeved shirt, to feel his hands on me.

Jeff stood around six feet tall, maybe an inch less, but bulky. Where Chase was a toned, proportionate specimen of male perfection, Jeff was more naturally powerful, heavy upper body and thick, muscular legs, all padded with a layer of softness that belied the power of his body. I'd seen him in action, breaking up fights in the bar, lifting hundred-pound speakers easily. He had short, thick brown hair, expressive dark brown eyes, almost black, and a broad, attractive face. He wasn't a handsome man, not classically beautiful like Chase was, but rather rugged, attractive in a rough-hewn way. Jeff wasn't much for words, but he managed to express a huge amount with a simple look, a quirk of the eyebrow, a small smile, a narrowing of the eyes.

We got the equipment set up, got the first songs worked through, and adjusted the quirks in the mix. Jeff and I did our first number together, "Summer Nights" from *Grease*. We always killed that one. Everyone loves that song. It's catchy, fun. The older crowd knows it from when the movie first aired, and the younger ones either know it or just like the poppy tune. Jeff's high, clear tenor suits the male part, and I can push my voice high enough to fit the female thread.

But the spark, the heat and tension driving that drove my performance with Chase...that wasn't there. It was just missing, and I couldn't sell the performance like I usually did with Jeff.

He noticed.

When we took our break in the closed, darkened bar kitchen, he followed me with a pair of Jaeger shots.

"You were flat at the end," he remarked, handing me my shot.

I downed it and gave him the rocks glass back. Jeff was blunt, and he always had been. I knew it, and it didn't usually bother me.

"Well, awesome," I snapped, feeling a sudden rush of irritation. "Thanks for that."

Jeff gave me a puzzled look. He tells me when I'm flat; I tell him.

"I didn't mean it like that, and you know it. Just letting you know." He muttered it, irritated.

"Well, next time keep your opinions to your goddamn self. I know when I'm flat."

"What the hell's your problem?"

"None of your fucking business, Jeff."

His eyes narrowed and his mouth turned down. The confused hurt on his face was palpable. I felt bad, knowing he'd done nothing to deserve my irritation.

"Jesus, Anna. Take a pill. Goddamn." He stuffed his phone back in his pocket and went back out into the bustle and noise of the bar.

Great, I thought. *Now I've pissed him off.*

The last thing I wanted to do was apologize, but I didn't want Jeff mad at me. He wouldn't say anything, just give me hard, sad glances and keep it to himself. It was worse than being yelled at.

I followed him out and cornered him behind the mixer. "Jeff, I'm sorry." My hand was on his arm; I hadn't meant to touch him, but now I couldn't move my hand away. "I'm being bitchy, and it's not your fault."

He shrugged, not looking at me directly, but over my shoulder. "No big. We all have bad days."

"Yeah, well, this may end up being more than a bad day, just fair warning." I didn't want to end up talking about it. "So if I'm a bitch to you, don't take it personally."

Jeff eyed me, then, a long, searching look. He had his suspicions what was bothering me, I think. He was too spare with his words and emotions to ask, though.

"We can talk about it after. I'll buy."

I shrugged, uncomfortable. I *did* want to talk about it, actually, but I wasn't sure Jeff was the right person.

"Maybe. We'll see. It's just one of those things, you know?"

Jeff lifted an eyebrow at my vague statement. "Well, the offer stands."

We made it through the night, and I managed to keep my irritability to a minimum. I only snapped at Jeff a few times.

When the customers were mostly gone and it was time to pack the equipment, Jeff waved me away.

"Go home, Anna. I got it."

Home. Jaime would be out still, over at her boyfriend's house, most likely. Silent, empty, lonely home.

I shook my head. "I'm fine. I'll help."

He rolled his eyes but let me carry the mixer to his SUV. When we'd finished loading, we bellied up to the bar and Darren, the owner and manager, slid us a pair of beers. We'd been DJing at Green's Tavern for years, and Darren let us stay after hours to drink until he had to leave.

We drank the first beer in companionable silence. Jeff spoke up halfway through the second.

"So. Problems with the boyfriend already, huh?" He spoke without looking at me, a Jeff-quirk.

"He wasn't my boyfriend." I *so* didn't want to get into the messy details. "Just a guy. But yeah. The problem is, he's gone."

Jeff took his time to formulate a response. "And you didn't want him to leave."

He was trying hard to hide the jealousy in his eyes, but he couldn't quite manage it. At least, not from me.

"It's complicated. It wasn't anything. Just one night. But then he had to leave, and he won't be back. Sucks."

Jeff spoke in short sentences, sometimes leaving out words. I had a tendency to start sounding like Jeff after a while.

"Sorry to hear it. He was good for you?"

Jeff was being careful. He knew I knew about his feelings for me, and he also knew I wasn't interested. What he didn't know was my mind and body seemed to be changing their minds.

"Yeah. He was great for me. Treated me like I was beautiful."

"That's 'cause you are." The words seemed to slip past his lips as if he'd tried to hold them back. "Shit." This last was mumbled into the mouth of his beer bottle.

I twisted on my stool to look at him. Our knees were almost touching, but not quite. I could feel the space between our knees as if static electricity was sparking between us.

"I am?" I tried not to make it sound flirty, but didn't succeed.

Jeff drained his beer and popped the top of the third. Darren had left a few on the bar for us while he counted the register. His actions were short and jerky, the bottle clinking against his teeth as he lifted it to his lips.

"Don't, Anna. Not if you don't mean it." He was examining the bar top as if it held an answer. "You know how I feel. So don't."

"How do you feel?" I wasn't looking at him, either. It was just easier.

Jeff didn't answer for a long time. "Quit playing games with me," he said, eventually.

I shifted my legs so our knees touched. Jeff jerked, as if the contact had physically shocked him.

"Damn it, Anna. Don't fuck with me." Jeff stood up and slammed his beer bottle down. "I need a shot, goddamn it."

"I'm not playing games, Jeff. I promise."

"Then what is this? What are you doing? I've spent six years as your friend and partner, nothing more. I haven't...what I feel hasn't changed in all that time. But now, suddenly...you?" Jeff reached over the bar and pulled a bottle of whiskey out, found a shot glass, and poured a finger into it; he slammed the shot, and then poured one for me. "Times like this I miss smoking."

He'd quit cigarettes two years before, and I'd never heard him voice a craving. He'd also never drank anything but beer or Jaeger.

Darren was at the end of the bar, watching us. He'd nodded at Jeff when he first grabbed the bottle. I was feeling dizzy now, but I didn't stop. I finished my beer and grabbed another. The dizziness was welcome, the lightheaded forgetting a pleasant distraction from my emotional turmoil.

Jeff was facing away from me, staring out the window into the darkness of an empty street, traffic light cycling from red to green.

"You're just using me as a crutch to get over what's-his-name," Jeff said, apropos of nothing. "Not fair to me."

I stood up unsteadily and made my way next to Jeff. I didn't touch him, although I wanted to.

"Maybe I'm just realizing what's been in front of me the whole time," I said.

"Horseshit," Jeff spat. "Besides, I don't want his leftovers."

Oh, ouch. I'm leftovers now?

"What the fuck, Jeff? I'm not sloppy seconds, I'm your friend. And I'm just wondering what else it might be, or could be. I don't know."

I turned away to stomp to my car, only I wobbled on my heels. Jeff caught me, and I shrugged him off. I was pissed off now, even though I knew Jeff was just pushing to protect himself.

"Fuck off, Jeff. I'm going home."

Jeff grunted in irritation and caught my arm again. "Not like this, you're not. You can barely walk. You aren't driving anywhere." He was both irritated and feeling his alcohol.

"I'm fine."

"You're not." Jeff pulled out his wallet, tossed a bill on the bar, and waved a goodbye to Darren. "I'll take you home. And Anna, I'm sorry. I didn't mean it. I was just pissed off."

I let him help me into the passenger seat of his Yukon. It smelled vaguely of pine-scented air freshener, and something that was indefinably Jeff-smell, clean and male. He leaned over me, buckled me in, dug in my purse for my keys, and locked my car. His presence in front of me had me inhaling his scent, wondering what the skin by his jaw tasted like.

Things were spinning, the dashboard wavering in front of my eyes, and the floor beneath my feet seemed to jump and wiggle.

"Guess I'm worse off than I thought," I said, hearing the slur. "Don't know what's come over me. I've done more shots than this and been fine."

Jeff snorted a laugh as he slid into the driver's seat and started the van. "You haven't eaten today. Your stomach's been growling since nine o'clock. Plus, you don't usually drink whiskey."

"What about you?" I focused on breathing and keeping my head straight on my shoulders.

"I'm fine."

I couldn't summon any more arguments. Maybe he was be fine, maybe he wasn't. I tried to remember how much he'd had, how much I'd had, but I couldn't; everything blurred together.

"Don't take me home," I mumbled. "Don't want to be alone."

Jeff glanced sidelong at me. "You can crash at my place."

I realized I'd never been to Jeff's place, and I didn't know if he lived in a house or an apartment. He drove slowly and carefully, seeming none the worse for wear. I was having trouble keeping track of time, and it might have been five minutes or an hour before we pulled up in front of a tiny house on a corner lot, deep in a subdivision. It was a shack more than anything, maybe one bedroom, if that.

Jeff helped me out and gestured to the house. "It's not much, but...well, it's home."

I slumped against him, letting him support my weight. I was feeling better than when I'd gotten into the car, but still dizzy. Jeff's arm was around my shoulders, and I let my head tilt to the side and rest on his arm. It was comforting, somehow familiar. He held me easily, and I didn't resist the urge to burrow into him. He smirked down at me, a lift of one side of his mouth, just a tipping of his lip, but it was enough to tell me he liked having his arm around me. It was a good start.

Inside, the house was tastefully decorated in light colors that made the tiny living room and galley kitchen seem bigger than I'd expected from the exterior. Jeff helped me lie down on the faded gray couch. It was deep, soft, and comfortable. I was tired all at once, my eyes heavy.

I was wearing a long skirt and boots, and the skirt was tangling between my legs and catching on my boot heels. I tugged at the boots, got one off, but the other defied my efforts. The zipper of my skirt was in the back, and I knew it was hopeless.

"Jeff, I need my other boot off."

He was gentle as he pulled the boot off my foot and set it neatly with the other by the door. He moved to cover me with a blanket, but I stopped him.

"I need the skirt off, too. It gets tangled."

Jeff's face contorted into something like panic. "I don't...your skirt? Can't you do that?"

I might have managed it if I stood up, but that wasn't happening. Plus, this was fun.

I twisted my hips to the side. "Please? I'll be more comfortable."

Jeff's jaw tightened, and one hand curled into a clenched fist before he uprooted himself and knelt beside me. His hand reached out, hovered over the zipper just above the swell of my backside. His eyes locked on mine; he wasn't afraid, or nervous, but I couldn't decipher the emotion in his eyes. Desire? Hesitation? Longing?

He took the zipper with precision, not so much as brushing the fabric, and drew it down, eyes riveted on my face.

He's proving something to me, I realized. *He won't touch me since I'm drunk.*

When the zipper was at the bottom, I lifted my hips, and he tugged the stretchy black fabric down, gripping near my legs where there was enough loose cotton to allow him to not touch me. The skirt slipped over my hips and he drew it off my feet, folded it, and set on the floor by my boots. He stood up, facing away from me.

Oh, no, you don't, I thought. He wasn't going to get away with not so much as looking at me.

"Jeff?"

"Hmmm?" He stopped and grunted the question without turning around.

"I'm thirsty." And I was, all of a sudden. Positively parched.

His shoulders slumped, and he shook his head. He filled a glass with water and brought it to me, keeping his eyes downcast until he reached the couch. His eyes met mine, flicked away, and then back.

When I'd gotten dressed, all I could find clean was a slinky purple thong, so that's what I was wearing. It barely covered me, even in front. I certainly hadn't had Jeff in mind when I'd put it on, but now I was grateful.

His eyes moved down to my low-cut T-shirt, which had hiked up to bunch just beneath my breasts, and down to my hips and legs.

"Goddamn, Anna. You're not making this easy on me."

"I'm not making what easy?" I asked.

"Being a gentleman."

"What if I don't want you to be a gentleman?"

Jeff closed his eyes and let out a long breath. "You're drunk."

"A little bit."

I kept my eyes on his and let him look. He fought it still, trying to focus on my eyes, but at last he gave in and let his gaze rove down my body, lingering on the minuscule patch of purple silk between the narrow "V" of my thighs. He turned away at last.

"Such a gentleman," I said, taking the glass from him and sitting up to drink it.

"I'm trying," he said, "but you're not making it easy. "

"Sorry," I said, but my tone of voice implied otherwise.

Jeff smirked. "No, you're not. You're just being difficult. Teasing me."

I faked a hurt look. "Me? A tease? Never." I smiled sweetly, all innocence. "I always follow through."

Jeff's eyes narrowed, and his hands twitched at his sides, as if trying to keep them from touching me.

"If you're playing a game with me, Anna, I swear, I'll never talk to you again. I mean it."

"I'm not playing a game. I promise." I finished the glass of water and set it on the coffee table before lying back down on the couch.

I only posed for Jeff a little bit.

He closed his eyes briefly before crouching next to me and drawing the blanket over my hips. His knuckles brushed along my skin from knee to hip bone, an electric spark crackling between us at the contact. I wanted him to run his hand up my leg, but he didn't. He seemed to think about it, though.

"Good night, Anna." He rose and went to his bedroom, closing the door behind him.

When I woke up, head pounding and stomach roiling, Jeff had a full breakfast spread out, eggs sunny-side up, bacon, toast, orange juice, coffee. I visited the bathroom, then meandered out to the kitchen.

"Thought you might be hungry." Jeff was sitting at his table, a round thing barely big enough for two people.

I slipped into the chair across from him, still basically naked from the waist down. The table was clear glass, and his gaze fell from my face to my legs. I pretended not to notice and dug in to the food, which was simple and delicious.

"Thanks for breakfast," I said.

"Welcome," Jeff grunted.

He got up and dug around in a cabinet, found a bottle of aspirin, and gave me two.

"And thanks for taking care of me last night," I added, swallowing the aspirin gratefully.

Jeff shrugged, uncomfortable. "That's what friends are for, I guess."

He drummed a rhythm on the glass with two fingers. I set my hand on his, just rested mine on top at first. When he glanced up at me in surprise, I slipped mine beneath his. His palm was warm and calloused on my hand, and he looked from our hands to my eyes and back.

His eyes burned into mine, questioning.

"Is that all we are?" I asked. "Just friends?"

Jeff looked at our hands again. "Well, it's all we have been." His eyes flicked up to mine. "Till now." It was almost a question, but not quite.

"Until now," I agreed.

I wasn't sure what this was, or where it was going, but I wanted to see. Jeff had been my friend for a long time, keeping his feelings for me on the down-low, never letting them interfere. He'd never tried anything, never asked me out, never told me he liked me or tried to seduce me. We'd gotten drunk together on a number of occasions, but he'd always been a perfect gentleman, just like last night. Only, last night I'd finally seen a glimpse of his desire for me.

So then, how did I know what he felt for me?

The little things. A look he would give me while setting up, meeting my gaze for a few beats too long, a wistful gleam in his eyes. The way he'd never let me do anything too hard, keeping all the heavy lifting for himself. Fending off drunks and keeping losers from hitting on me.

I looked at him, at the slope of his shoulders and the tension in his eyes. He was waiting for this to end, for me to tell him we'd just be friends. He'd never tried anything with me, but he wanted to.

"Jeff? Can I ask you something?"

"You just did, didn't you?" He smirked, that rare little expression of humor.

"You know what I meant." He lifted a shoulder, and I plunged ahead. "Why haven't you ever tried anything? As more than friends, I mean?"

A long silence, and then a shrug of one shoulder. It wasn't even an answer, but somehow there was a wealth of expression in it. The shrug seemed to mean hidden fear, worry of rejection, a whole slew of things he could and would never say aloud, or even admit to himself in so many words.

"You never know until you try, right?"

Jeff opened his mouth to speak, but closed it again. After a deep breath, he tried again. "I didn't mean what I said last night, but I do have to know. Why now?"

"Sometimes...you just wake up one day and see what's always been there."

"I guess." He threaded his fingers through mine, a gesture of finally giving in to hope.

He seemed about to say something else, but he shook his head, drew his hand out of mine, and stood up.

"I'm gonna take a shower. I won't be long," he said, and then he was gone.

I heard the bathroom door closing and the shower start, and I was left sitting alone, wondering why he'd pulled away. He'd seemed on the verge of something but had swerved aside.

I knew he wanted me, I'd seen that last night. So...maybe it was up to me? Maybe he wouldn't believe I actually wanted him unless I showed him, in no uncertain terms.

Why shouldn't I go after him? His hand brushing my leg had been electric, thrilling. What would sex be like? Even more electrifying, likely.

There's only one way to find out.

My body was moving before my brain was aware of the decision being made. At some point, my shirt ended up on the floor, leaving me clad only in a front-clasp bra and thong.

The bathroom door was unlocked. My heart was pitter-pattering in my chest as I entered the steam-clouded bathroom. His shower door was clear glass, fogged by steam but still translucent enough to show me his body, thick and heavily muscled. His manhood was limp and pointing down;

from what I could see, it would be enormously thick. I wanted a better, closer look. I wanted to touch, to taste. Desire was pooling in my belly, and it wasn't only for release, for relief from the sexual frustration raging through me, but for Jeff, for the man I'd worked with for so long, knew so well, but didn't know at all, in some ways.

He must have heard the door creak open. "Damn it, Anna. I'm in the shower."

"I like the way you say that. So irritated, but still affectionate. 'Damn it, Anna.'"

"What are you doing in here? I'll be done soon."

He wasn't turning away but wasn't moving to open the door, either. I crossed the tiny bathroom in one step, slid the stall door open. He was beautiful, in his own way. His body wasn't sculpted, but it was still hugely muscled, his arms as thick as my thighs, his stomach not flat, but slightly rounded and hard as a boulder. His legs were massive, thighs like ancient oak trees.

His cock twitched at the sight of me. His thick, short brown hair was pasted to his head as water sluiced onto his shoulders and poured down his body. I stood and let him look, taking in the view of his body, my tongue running over my lower lip in appreciation for his physique.

"I'm sober. You don't need to be a gentleman this time."

"Why?" He was still fighting the urge to stare.

"Does it matter?"

"Yes. It does to me."

My legs were being spattered by the shower. I waited for him to move, thinking about his question. Why now?

"I guess I just realized what I wanted. I don't know." His eyes were raking my body now, lingering on my breasts; I stepped closer, nearly in the shower now. "That's the best answer I can give you right now. I don't know."

"What do you want, then?" He hadn't moved toward me, but he looked like he was on the verge of it.

"You." The word came out of me in a whisper.

"Me." He shuffled forward a half-step, his hand lifting for me. "You're sure? This is a line we can't uncross."

I just nodded and took a deep breath, swelling my breasts in my bra. Jeff was semi-rigid now, pointing straight forward. I let myself look, let him see me looking. He rested one hand on my waist at first, a hesitant, questing touch. I moved closer, and his body blocked the spray of water. He was hardening with every passing moment. I kept my hands at my sides.

Both of his hands were on the concave curve of my waist now and sliding up, rivulets of hot water dripping down my sides. Up farther, then, closer to my breasts. He met my eyes, still hesitating.

"I'm not going to change my mind." I unclasped my bra and set it aside. "Touch me."

He was fully erect now, and I couldn't help comparing him to Chase, just for a moment. He wasn't as long as Chase, but he was thicker, and perfectly straight, whereas Chase had been slightly curved.

I wanted to take him in my hands, but I kept still, waiting for Jeff's hands to finish their upward journey and heft my breasts in his large hands.

"Don't play me, Anna." His voice was low and husky, his hands stopped on my ribcage.

"Oh, for god's sake." I closed the gap between us and pressed my lips to his.

He was startled, frozen for a moment, then he softened into the kiss and dipped his tongue past my teeth. His kiss was gentle, achingly tender for such a hard, gruff man. His calloused palms caught the undersides of my tits and cupped them. His murmur of pleasure buzzed against my sternum. I put my hands on his shoulders and ran them down his back to curl around his hard, round ass. At my touch to his backside, Jeff pressed into me, crushing his erect shaft between us.

I stepped back, pushed Jeff into the shower, and stripped off my thong before joining him. Now I touched his cock for the first time, wrapping one hand around him, slicking a thumb across his bulbous, leaking tip.

Oh, my sweet lord, I thought, clutching his cock with greedy hunger, *he's huge. SO thick. He would fill me, and then some.*

He rumbled again, one corner of his mouth tipping up in a smile, his eyes half-closed. My hair was still in a ponytail and I tugged it free, letting the stream of scalding water wet my hair against my scalp and neck. Jeff ran his hands across my face, brushing sopping strands of hair away from my face, and down the back of my head. His hand rested on the nape of my neck and pulled me into a kiss. My hand was still fisted around his thickness, and I kept enough distance between our hips to allow myself room for stroking. He was at once soft and hard, a skin of silk around a core of steel.

My breathing was turning to sighing gasps as I felt him throb in my fist, felt his hips pump him into my hand. His fingers found my nipples, hard and sensitive, sending zaps of arousal thrilling through my body. One hand kept toying with my nipple, and the other circled my waist to clutch my ass, caressing, digging into the muscle and flesh, caressing again, spanning the crease to grasp the other cheek.

All this with the delicious heat of the water dousing us, wrapping us in warmth.

"I can't believe you're here in my shower with me," Jeff said.

"Me, neither," I said, "but there's nowhere else I'd rather be."

"You're sexy." Jeff's fingers descended the plain of my belly to skim over the hillock of my pussy as he spoke, stroking the entrance with a single finger. "So goddamn sexy. Come for me, Anna."

I leaned back against the wall and out of the stream of water, spreading my thighs apart to allow him access. He was the perfect height to take me like this.

"Make me," I told him.

He didn't answer, just pressed his lips to the mound of one breast, lapped his tongue down the wet surface to flick against the taut bead of my nipple. I pressed my palm against his iron-hard neck, pushing his mouth deeper around my breast. His other finger continued the teasing exploration of my pussy, tracing the lines of the labia, tickling the crease between my leg and hip, dipping in between my thighs to streak across my perineum.

He penetrated me at last, one gentle, questing finger into my aching channel. I clenched my buttocks and arched my hips forward, and he skinned the inner walls with his finger before pulling out to furrow against the nub of my clit. I gasped as he touched me there, eyes closed and whispering "yes" with an inbreath. Two fingers then, slipping back in and exploring my pussy, retreating out, grazing my clit, and then three fingers.

My hips were moving, my hands gripping his cock as a handle, holding on to him as I pushed into his fingers. Pressure was rising, now, magma welling in my belly, surging up to ready for a volcanic eruption. His fingers stoked the heat, one finger in, curling to slash across my G-spot, eliciting a moan that echoed in the shower. Two fingers again, pulling out of my pussy to dovetail around my clit, pinching it, slipping back and forth.

His other hand was busy with my breasts, pinching and rolling my nipples, teeth now nipping the rippled skin of my areola, tongue laving the sides and across my chest and ribcage.

Finally he set a rhythm, three fingers diving in and back out, pressing onto my clit with every stroke. One small quiver in my belly at first, a buckle of the knees into his upstroke. My hands, slipping up and down on his manhood now, slow pumps around his swollen, straining head.

Another stutter, lower down, a swelling tremor pushed into a rolling waveform. Jeff sped the rhythm of his fingers' plunge, billowing the heaving of my hips into a desperate gyration. Then he slowed, just before the upwelling explosion overtook me.

"Faster, please, faster," I breathed.

He complied, surging faster, biting my nipples and using both hands on me now, two fingers circling my nub, three fingers diving in. My hips were moving on their own now, pulsing upward. My hands worked his shaft in time with my hips' motion, and then...

Every muscle buckled and tensed as my long-pent orgasm finally coursed through me, a rocketing surge of heat and ecstasy in my belly, pussy muscles clamping around his frenzied fingers, his mouth on my neck and lips and tits, my feet lifting me up and dropping me down.

"Inside," I gasped. "I need you...inside me."

"Don't have protection," he breathed against my breast.

"On...pill," I said. I couldn't form full sentences.

Jeff's arms curled up around my ass, and then one hand lifted my leg by the knee. I guided him into me, leaning into his body, the shower spray, growing lukewarm now, blasting against my neck and the top of his head. He pulsed into me, a slow, careful thrust.

"Goddamn, Anna. You're so tight."

I opened my mouth to tell him it was just because he was so huge, but he thrust again and I could only gasp, breathless, as my pussy stretched to fit him. My labia formed an "O" of taut-stretched flesh, burning and throbbing so wonderfully, my orgasm still pounding through me, constricting my inner muscles around his thick, slick member.

His thrusts timed with the contracting pulsations of my orgasm.

"Oh, god, Jeff, yes…" I scraped the words past rasping vocal chords.

Every fiber of my being quivered; my eyelids fluttered, my thighs trembled, my fingers clawed down his broad back, my toes curled in, my breath caught on an inbreath and held; a plunge, and I came again, riding the crest of the last explosion, another plunge, and I came again, clutching to Jeff with all my waning strength.

He never sped his thrusts, held himself to slow, measured pushes, going deeper with each one.

"Anna." He grated my name past clenched teeth as he came, thrusting hard and deep to the rhythm of my name. Two syllables, a full thrust inward on the initial emphasis, our hips bumping together on the "N," retreating on the outbreath "A."

I felt his seed hit my inner walls, felt him throb within me as he continued to come, and come and come, lips crushed to my shoulder. He held my leg firm around his hip all the while, pulled on my knee for leverage, his free hand roaming my torso, breast to belly and back up, fingering my hypersensitive nipples.

The water was going cold now, and he finally let my leg down and pulled out of me. I shut the water off and pulled him against me, curling into his heat, our damp skin sticking together, our breathing matched gasps.

He moved away first, pulled a thick white towel from a rack and spread it open, drew me out of the shower. What he did next made my breath hitch. He scrubbed every inch of my body with the towel, beginning with my shoulders and moving down my back, across my belly, around each breast, my arms and sides, then my buttocks and thighs, down my legs and back up. The last thing he did was gently spread my thighs apart and clean my tender folds, wiping carefully downward and in to clean me of his still-leaking essence, his touch featherlight and almost reverent.

I couldn't help but do the same. Another dry towel hung on the rack, and I rubbed it across his muscles, cupping his sack and massaging his flaccid member with it. It was a moment both tender and erotic, and I didn't know what to do with it.

I followed him to his bedroom, a tiny space filled with a queen-sized bed and a low dresser, and nothing else. No pictures, no posters or paintings or anything. The window was open, letting the brilliant noonday sunlight stream in, bathing everything yellow-white. The bed was neatly made already, the corners crisp, the blanket tucked in under the pillow in a line as straight as razor. On the dresser was a wide, shallow metal dish, filled with loose change, a single bullet shell, and a battered set of dog tags.

I sat on the edge of the bed, naked, still trembling

from the aftershocks. Jeff stood in front of me, looking down at me with an inscrutable expression on his face. He was just out of arm's reach, hands at his sides, his posture relaxed, but his gaze was intense, focused on me, sweeping and searching.

"What?" I asked.

He shook his head and closed the distance between us, standing between my knees. His cock was right at eye-level, point down and seeming to be waiting for me to touch it. I looked up at him, gave him a smile as I put my hands on his hips, traced the line of the muscles on his thighs.

I dragged my fingernail down the outside of his thigh and back up the inside edge to his groin. I watched his eyes as I traced my finger from the very bottom of his sack upward, feeling the skin tighten under the pad of my finger, and then lifted his cock with my finger, tracing its length as well. His gaze was fiery, dark eyes glittering. His hands rested on my shoulders, not pushing or pulling, just touching me.

I ran my fingernail down his cock again, this time from the root against his belly down to the tip, then scratched the tip with my nail. The flesh of his cock was tightening, but he wasn't growing hard yet. He hadn't sprung into an instant erection, and I found myself enjoying the process of touching Jeff during his refractory period, learning the way his body looked and felt.

I scooched back on the bed and moved to one side, patting the blanket beside me. He hesitated, then climbed up on the bed beside me. As he turned his back to me, ever so briefly, I saw the reason for the long-sleeved shirts. He'd been burned badly on his back, shoulders, and arms, running down to his elbows and across one forearm.

He saw me notice. "Car accident, years ago."

I rolled to lay my head on his chest, and his arm snaked around my body to cup the curve of my hip, resting there with familiar, tender affection.

"What happened?" I asked.

He blew air through puffed-out cheeks. "Long story. My buddy and I were driving the Seeney Stretch, up in the UP. Hit a deer, flipped a couple times. I was in the passenger seat. Got tossed out of the car, which prolly saved my life. Well, my buddy Brett wasn't so lucky. Got trapped under the car when it stopped rolling upside down. I was panicked. I'd known Brett all my life. Had to get him out, so I tried to flip the car on my own. I did, too. Adrenaline rush, that kinda thing. Flipped it over so I could drag Brett out. Problem is, I was pushing on the bottom of the car, where things were hot. Burned me pretty bad."

That was the most I'd ever heard Jeff say all at once in my life.

"Did your friend..."

Jeff just shook his head and I let it go, turning

my attention to sliding my palms along his body, fingertips exploring the heavy, undefined bulk of his muscles. I realized he was much bigger than I'd ever thought. His shirts made him seem smaller somehow, but in reality, he would be much, much stronger than Chase.

"I'm sorry to hear that," I replied, belatedly.

"Long time ago." He shrugged, and turned his gaze to my body, nestled naked against his.

Our warm flesh merged in one long point of contact. I felt comfortable there, held in his arms. Safe. The oddest thing was, even post-sex, still naked and feeling his hot skin and hard muscle, I felt just as at ease with Jeff as if we were setting up for a shift at The Dive.

His palm moved from the swell of my hip to the hollow of my waist, then down to graze my ass, curling around one cheek and hefting it, following the crease down to the fold where ass meets thigh and then moved back up my body. He rolled so I landed on my back, supporting his head on his elbow. His free hand continued its slow exploration of my body, leaving nowhere untouched. He circled my kneecap, up the inside of my thigh, dipped into my navel and the sides of my belly, my ribs; he spent forever on my breasts, lingering on every square inch of skin.

At last, at long last, he moved his attention downward, tickling my belly, my thighs, and finally slipping one long index finger to the keyhole gap of my pussy. I moved my legs apart, greedy for his touch, hungry to be stimulated, turned on, toyed and played with and sated. He didn't touch me to bring me to climax, at first. It was the same way he touched the rest of my body, as if...as if memorizing my body, creating a mental map of my curves to remember.

"You're beautiful, Anna." The way he said it, his voice was softer than I ever remember him speaking, a world away from the gruff voice he used most of the time.

It was three words, but coming from Jeff it was worth ten thousand words. He was spare with words, to the point where sometimes getting him to use complete sentences could be a chore, like dragging answers from a teenager.

"Thank you."

He gave me his Jeff smile, the upward quirk of one corner of his mouth, just a twitch of the muscles, but a smile nonetheless.

I leaned up and kissed him, a slow meeting of lips, a gradual exploration of mouth-space with tongues. His arm wrapped around my back and pulled me closer, rolled me to my side facing him. One arm was trapped between us, and I used that one to touch his manhood, stiffening now under my caress. My other hand slipped up his back and rested between his shoulder blades, stayed there.

Encouraging his cock to full girth was a slow process, deliberately so. I could have used my mouth to speed it up, but I enjoyed just touching him, holding him, feeling its weight in my hand, brushing the tip in slow, small circles, cupping his balls in my palm, sliding up his length and back down in lazy dips and rises, twisting around him in spirals.

I wasn't even aware of movement, of a change of position. I blinked, breathed, and found Jeff above me, kneeling between my thighs, his hands on either side of my face, his flinty near-black eyes soft on mine, searching my face.

I didn't need to guide him in with my hands. He found my entrance without taking his eyes from me, as if his body knew exactly where to merge with mine. He slipped inside me with exquisite slowness, utter gentility, as if I were delicate. In the shower, he'd claimed me slowly, but his desire had been there beneath the surface, boiling within him like magma surging to the core of a volcano; he'd forced himself to go slow, as if savoring the experience.

Now, he went slow out of pure desire to simply take his time, in no rush, no hurry. He dipped down and kissed me, his tongue flicking out to meet mine in the rhythm of his hips' lunges against mine. My arms floated up as if borne on unfelt winds to snake around his neck as he kissed me;

he slipped one thick forearm beneath my head as a pillow, and with his other hand cupped and caressed my breasts, whisking his palms across my nipples, tweaking them, circling and lifting and squeezing, as if he could never get enough of touching them.

All the while, his slow, inexorable thrusting into me continued, his breathing unchanging, his eyes locked on mine when we weren't kissing. And, just because it was Jeff, he was silent.

Then, when the fluttering of climax began in my belly, and I moaned in his ear and wrapped my legs around his waist, he allowed himself one barely audible "mmmmm" in my ear, and then another when I dug my nails into his back.

He slowed then. Just when my climax began and his neared, he slowed, dragged it out. He wrapped his other arm under my head with the first, and now his thrusts were merely at the surface, barely entering, shallow dips, quick plunges, and back out. I whined high in my throat, protesting the change. He only kissed me, and then plunged deep, once, drawing a gasp from me. Back to flutters, then, kissing me at each thrust, touch of the lips and thrust, again and again, his tongue darting between my lips each time.

The deepest stroke yet, then, burying himself inside me, his voice buzzing "mmmmmm" in my ear, his breath on my cheek. Again, and deeper.

Oh, lord, another plunge, deeper and so slow. A rhythm, then back to the exquisitely slow strokes, deeper than ever, hips grinding at each apex.

The only sound was our breathing, an occasional whimper, a soft "mmmmmm" from Jeff; sunlight streaks across our bodies, bright and hot.

The climax rose, brought from a small flutter to a sudden hot impending pressure, a kind of crushing need in my belly, deep inside me. This was like nothing I'd ever experienced. He took his time, pulsing into me, building up to the peak in steady blocks of pleasure, backing away from the edge each time, but not enough to allow us to slip back down and lose the burning need for release.

I couldn't have said how long he'd been above me, tireless and supporting his weight so no part of him rested on me. Minutes? Days? I didn't know, and didn't care. The unhurried pace was delicious, each stroke filling me completely, each thrust delivering wondrous pleasure throughout me.

I knew, when the climax came, it would be blinding in its intensity, would carry on for an eternity. I had no doubt he would bring me there in his own time, and I was perfectly content to let him take me there.

Slow strokes, deep and gentle, were replaced by longer, harder thrusts after a time. I wrapped my legs around his ass again, pulled him against me at each thrust.

He wrapped an arm around my leg, and then the other, and he was supporting his weight on my legs, kneeling above me, driving so deep, deeper than I'd ever been taken, so perfectly, incredibly deep, I thought perhaps he might lose himself inside me, and it struck me that perhaps this was exactly his desire, to bury himself within me and never leave.

In that moment, I wouldn't have argued.

The climax erupted then, with my legs near his chest, held by his arms. It wasn't a sudden detonation —it was an inevitable overwhelming flood tide, washing through me not in waves but in a gradual up-surging. Our pace increased, but imperceptibly, until he was driving into me with relentless speed, but still gentle, never pounding.

"God, yes," I whispered, my first words since we began. "More."

He released my legs and curled over me, and I wrapped my arms and legs around him, clung to him, held tight to him as he found his release, and now I came with him. It wasn't hard, or explosive, or shattering. It was an intense falling into perfection, a coming home.

When he lay next to me once more, I pillowed my head on his chest, felt his arms wrap around me, and fell into the deepest, most restful slumber of my life.

It was late evening when I woke up, facing away from Jeff, with his arm around my belly. His erection was a hard lump between my ass cheeks, and I knew by his breathing he was awake.

I'd never before woken up aroused, but in that moment I felt a rush of dampness hit my pussy and drip through me, my nipples standing on end. I pushed my ass into him, took his hand and brought it to my breast. He writhed his cock into me, caressing my breast.

I rolled to my stomach and rose up on my forearms and knees. "Take me like this," I said.

Jeff rose up to his knees behind me, palmed my ass with both hands and spread me apart, and now I felt the first touch of his tongue to my sex, an erotically slow lick up the length of my pussy, followed by another, each striking deeper, starting at my nub and moving upward to my perineum. Each swipe of his tongue had my hips bucking, had me rocking forward and back into him.

Gentle and slow and relentless and methodical, this was his way, bringing me to a gasping, whimpering climax in a puddle on the bed. Then he entered me, dipping a finger into me and following it with his cock and driving deep. I was collapsed on my face, still shuddering from the first orgasm when he drove into me, and I immediately, automatically rose back up to push back into him.

What I wanted then was for him to lose himself in me, to make him forget the gentility. I wanted his pleasure in me to be…rapturous, a turnaround for the way he'd so carefully brought me to climax.

I rocked backward into every thrust, moaning with each motion.

"Yes, Jeff, yes," I said, "Take me, take me hard."

"Don't wanna hurt you," he grunted.

He was moving faster now, gliding into me with his hands on my back, pulling me into him.

"You won't, I promise."

I slammed my ass into him, forcing him deeper, and again, and now he was beginning to lose control, growling low his throat, a long rumble as he pushed into me.

"Yes, yes," I gasped, "Just like this. God, yes, it feels so good."

He was gripping my hips now, jerking me onto his cock, all technique abandoned, moving furiously. The explosions began, going from zero to full bore within seconds, from devouring his cock and loving it to frenzied orgasm within the space of a single thrust.

He came into me, clawing his fingers down my spine, thrusting slow and so wonderfully hard, my tits bouncing. His seed filled me, a hot jet spurting throughout me, drilled harder and deeper as he continued to climax.

I was shrieking with every thrust of his cock into me, sometimes whimpering his name, sometimes a wordless wail of ecstasy. His crushing thrusts slowed finally and he withdrew, pulling me down back into his arms.

"Goddamn, Anna. You make me feel so good," Jeff said, breathless.

I rolled into him, kissed him hard and full of passion. "*So* good. *So* good."

Silence, filled with our hands exploring each other's bodies, an almost idle survey of skin.

"I'm hungry," Jeff said. "How about some dinner?"

Maggiano's was busy, humming with subdued energy. It was a Saturday night, and from what I knew, you had to have reservations to get a table here on the weekends, but somehow Jeff had managed it.

I stood next to him as we waited for the host. He was dressed simply, in blue jeans and a crisp, spotless white button-down, plain brown leather belt and polished dress shoes, but he made it look formal, almost dressy. I realized again how attractive he really was.

When the host led us to our booth, Jeff's hand found my skin between my shoulder blades where my dress left my back bare, and even that small amount of contact left me trembling. A gentle, casual touch, but it was enough to make me want to feel his hand brushing down my back, sweeping across my naked backside again...

My sexual frustration was gone, but in its place was a raging, insatiable hunger. Now that I'd felt Jeff, had him, been in his bed and experienced his slow, thorough plundering, I couldn't get enough.

His dark eyes roved the restaurant, his big, warm hand holding mine gently. His presence next to me, his hand in mine...it felt natural, easy, and comfortable. But at the same time there was a sense of nerves in my belly, nerves and something else, a burning, fluttering of desire. His eyes found mine and my heart pattered, thumping in anticipation.

We sat side by side in the booth, the light low and soft yellow, conversation from other tables washing over us in a dull blur of sound, Frank Sinatra and Ella Fitzgerald filling the spaces. We drank expensive wine, lingered over soup and salad, knees brushing, me asking questions and him answering in his typically spare way. I learned he'd been in the Army for four years, done two tours in Iraq and been stationed in the Philippines after. He skipped over the Army bit, saying only that he'd been a grunt, seen combat, and then clammed up. I could tell he didn't want to talk about it. I knew if I asked, he'd tell me, but he'd rather I didn't ask.

As we ate, I let my hand wander underneath the table to rest on his thigh. I was feeling...daring. At first, I left my fingers on his leg, but, over the space of several minutes, let it drift incrementally higher until Jeff lifted an amused and surprised eyebrow. He gasped audibly when I moved my hand high enough to feel his package, a thick lump even through the denim of his jeans. A few subtle zipping strokes of my hand on his groin had him hardening under my touch.

"What are you doing, Anna?" Jeff whispered to me.

"Doing? Nothing. What am I doing?"

He growled, a low grunt of irritation, arousal, and amusement. "Teasing me."

I circled my palm on him, felt him get hard enough to need adjusting. I tucked my fingers in the waistband of his jeans and pulled them away, allowing his erection to spring vertical.

"Teasing?" I ran my tongue over my bottom lip, stroking his denim-covered length underneath the table. "I never tease. I make promises."

"Promises. I'll bet." He squirmed in his seat, fully erect now. "We're in the middle of a restaurant. How're you going to keep this promise?"

I smirked at him, mimicking his tipping of one side of his mouth. "I didn't say *when* I would keep my promise, just that I would. And I will."

"Well, I call that teasing." Jeff's eyes twinkled, and the corners of his eyes crinkled, worth more than an outright laugh from any other, more verbose, kind of man. "And two can play that game."

We were done with dinner, sopping up the last of the pink vodka sauce from our plates with focaccia bread; our server came by with a tray of desserts.

"Did you save room for dessert?" Our server was a young man with a faux-hawk and a carefully trimmed goatee.

At that very moment, when the server approached and directed his question at me, Jeff slipped his fingers under my dress, between my thighs, and into my pussy, all in one sudden motion. My eyes flew wide and I gasped. Jeff's face remained impassive as he fingered my clit in slow strokes.

"Ma'am? Are you alright?" The server's brow furrowed in worry; my gasp had been sharp, a surprised intake of breath.

"Yeah...I just...oh...stubbed my toe on the... the table leg." Fortunately for my excuse, there was a central bar holding the table up.

"Are you all right?"

I stifled another gasp as Jeff sped his finger's attention to my wet, sensitive nub. "Yeah, yeah I'm fine."

"So, dessert?" He pointed at the various items

on the dessert tray: New York-style cheesecake, lemon cookies, apple crostada, crème brûlée, tiramisu, and spumoni...

I stopped listening when he got to spumoni, although to be honest, I only heard half of what he said anyway. My brain was scrambled by Jeff's strong, relentless finger circling my clit, by the need to stifle my usually vocal reaction to my rising climax. I was so close that my thighs were trembling, and I was using every shred of my self-control to not undulate my hips into his hand.

"Ma'am? Would you like to make a dessert selection?" The server was getting antsy and confused by my vacant, distracted behavior.

"Order what you want, Anna," Jeff said. "I'll eat whatever."

"I'll have...ahem?" I was reaching climax now, and speech was nearly impossible. "Crème brûlée, please." I wasn't sure I liked crème brûlée, couldn't remember ever having it; my mouth spouted an answer that completely bypassed my brain.

"Very good, ma'am," the server said, and then he was gone, thank goodness.

I slumped down in the booth, breathing through my nose in long, controlled huffs, fists clenched tight, nails digging into my palms, fire pooling in my belly and crashing through my body...

...and then Jeff stopped, withdrew his hand, and left it on my thigh.

"Goddamn it, Jeff!" I spoke through gritted teeth, wanting to scream in frustration. "Not fair!"

"Turnabout's fair play." The humor was in Jeff's voice, in the subtle softening of the corners of his mouth, the almost imperceptible lift of one eyebrow.

"Well, *that's* not cliché."

"I wasn't *teasing*, Anna. I was making a *promise*."

"Oh, you bastard."

"Don't tease me, I won't tease you," Jeff said. His finger brushed between my thighs again, and they split open on their own, with alacrity. "But if you ask nicely, I may finish what I started."

I grabbed his hand and tugged it higher, toward my wet, aching opening. "Please, Jeff?" I used my tiniest, most innocent voice. "I'm sorry. I won't ever tease you again."

Jeff smiled, both sides of his mouth lifting this time; a real, bona fide grin. I felt victorious, having wrested a full-fledged smile from a man so taciturn as Jeff Cartwright.

"I'm not sure you'll keep that promise, but I'll go easy on you this time." His finger brushed the fabric of my thong aside and delved into me. "But you have to be quiet. I wouldn't want to be embarrassed."

I gasped and fluttered my eyes. Of course, the server came up with my crème brûlée at that very moment. He only eyed me this time, frowning in puzzlement.

"Will there be anything else?" the server asked. He had our dessert in one hand, and the tray in another, presumably to show another table.

"I think I'd like to take a look at the desserts, actually, now that I've seen Anna's," Jeff said.

Jeff was circling my clit now, wringing a climax from me in record time. I forced myself to hold still, to keep my ass planted in the seat and my mouth shut. Miniscule whimpers kept escaping me, though, and the server was giving me increasingly perplexed glances as he pointed out and described each dessert.

"And what's in the tiramisu?" Jeff asked.

My teeth were grinding so hard my jaw ached, my fingernails were digging into my palms hard enough to draw blood, and I was exploding from the inside out, tongues of fire blossoming from my sex up through my belly and into my thighs and chest and down to my toes, curling them in my strappy platform sandals. If I were in a bedroom, I would be shrieking, moaning, clutching to Jeff for dear life as I rode the wave of ecstasy. Instead, I sat, still and silent, pitiful whimpers drifting from my lips at intervals as Jeff listened to the server patiently described ladyfinger pastries soaked in espresso, layered with blah blah blah OH GOD help me he wasn't stopping, surely he felt my muscles clenching around the fingers he'd slipped in and up to my G-spot, surely he knew I was coming, dying, but no, he kept stroking, kept pushing me higher.

A wave rocked through me, and I couldn't stop the gasp from escaping. To cover, and to mollify the server's concerned expression, I faked a cough. Which then turned into a real cough, and now Jeff *and* the server were looking at me in concern. I took a sip from one of the glasses of ice water, the ice now melted and the glass covered in dripping sweat. I put the glass to my lips, and a took generous mouthful of lukewarm water. What did Jeff do? He slipped his finger out of my pussy and explored backward, past the stretch of skin and pressed onto my second, tighter opening.

I spewed water all over the server. I mean I sprayed it all over the front of his apron, his shirt and tie, his order book...everywhere. How *humiliating*.

Jeff actually, factually chuckled. A real laugh. At my expense, sure, but a laugh. It was almost worth the embarrassment. He stifled the chuckle with a sip of wine.

When I'd quit hacking enough to breathe again, I muttered an apology. "Sorry, it went down the wrong pipe."

The server looked disgusted, wiping ineffectually at himself with a napkin that had been dangling from his back pocket. He turned and walked away without so much as glancing at me or Jeff, still trying to dry himself off. When he was gone, I rounded on Jeff, my eyes blazing.

"What the hell was that?" I demanded.

Jeff just smirked at me. "I didn't want to leave you hanging."

Not like I had him, was the implication.

"But did you have to do it with the server there?" I squirmed in my seat, still feeling the aftershocks, and the surprise of his finger in my asshole. "And you *really* didn't have to put your finger *there*?"

Jeff retained his innocently blank expression. "Where?"

"You know where." I leaned close, feeling more shy than I'd ever been; I'm not a shy girl. "You stuck your finger in my ass. That's why I spat water all over that poor server."

"I did? Gee, Anna, I'm sorry." Jeff's tone belied his words. He was all but laughing out loud. He knew exactly what he'd done. "Didn't you like it? You seemed like you did. I would never do anything you didn't like." That last sentence was delivered with an intense sincerity, all joking aside.

"No, I did like it, honestly. It just surprised me. I've never been touched there." I kissed his jaw and whispered in his ear. "I wouldn't mind if you did it again later, in private."

Jeff nodded, as if filing the information away for later. "Your crème brûlée is getting cold."

I giggled. "I just said the first thing that came to mind. I don't even know if I'll like it. I was a little...distracted."

It turned out I did like crème brûlée, and so did Jeff. Jeff paid the bill, ignoring my attempts to help pay it, and we left.

We got to Jeff's house, which wasn't far from my place. Sexual tension filled the car, the smell of my arousal musky and intense. I wanted to touch Jeff, to feel him fill my hand, but he wouldn't let me. He held my hand in a firm grip on his thigh, a safe distance away from his crotch.

"I'd rather wait until we can do things right," was all he said.

I managed to wait until we were inside and Jeff was kicking off his shoes to attack him. I sidled up behind him and pulled at the buckle of his belt, and then worked my way down the button-fly of his jeans. He slipped his shoes aside and straightened, putting his hands behind him on my hips. His head tipped back as I pushed his pants and boxers down to let his still-rising erection free. I wrapped eager fingers around him, the other hand cupping his sack and stroking the skin behind it.

Still cradling his balls in one hand, I caressed his length as lightly as I could, focusing my ministrations on his tip until the first pearls of moisture began to leak from him. I smeared my palm along his tip, and felt his knees buckle as I did so.

I circled around in front of him, pushed him backward to the couch until his knees hit and he sat down. I knelt in front of him and pulled his jeans and boxers off, and then settled between his knees.

"Anna, you don't have to, just because I—"

"I want to," I cut in. "I want to taste you. I want to feel you come like this."

He didn't argue. I took him in both hands, pushing down on him in a hand-over-hand cycle. When his breath started to come in gasps and his hips began to move, I leaned forward and fit him into my mouth. I had to stretch my jaw as wide as it would go to take him. He smelled and tasted clean and of male musk. His skin was salty and slick and smooth. I started a slow bob of my head, careful not to graze him with my teeth. He leaned his head back against the couch and tangled his fingers in my hair, not pulling or tugging, merely holding. One hand pumping him at the base, I slipped my hand underneath him and put my middle finger to the stretch of skin behind his balls and pushed, gently, as he began to move his hips. He was struggling to keep still. I lowered my head to take him deeper until he brushed the back of my throat, feeling him throb harder against my lips. His body tensed as I drew him out and wrapped my lips around his head, working him with my hand and sucking hard. My cheeks hollowed and he gasped a shuddering breath, arched his back, and tightened his grip on my hair.

"I'm coming, oh, god..." His warning accompanied the jet of viscous, salty come against the back of my throat.

As soon as I felt him tense and climax, I put a second finger to his taint and massaged in circles, lips on his head, hand pumping in a blur. He shot a second time, and then a third, his back arched in a rigid curve.

When he finally went limp, I let him go and sat on the couch next to him, resting my hand on his belly.

"God, you come a lot," I said.

"Sorry," he said.

I laughed. "It's not a bad thing," I said. "I don't mind."

"Thank you," Jeff said. "That was...incredible. It's been a long time since I've...never mind."

"What?" I put my head on his shoulder and looked up at him. "A long time since what?"

"Since I've had that done to me."

"Do you like it?"

"Well, yeah, obviously. Like I said, it was amazing. But now it's your turn."

He stood and pulled me to my feet, drawing me

into his bedroom. He kissed me as he unzipped my dress and let it fall to the ground around my feet, and we got lost for a few minutes, clinging to each other and kissing.

"I could kiss you forever," Jeff said. He unhooked my bra, kissing my shoulder as he slipped the straps off.

He nudged me onto the bed, stripping my panties off as he did so, and then he was kneeling above me, staring down at me with an expression on his face telling me more clearly than any words how beautiful he thought I was. I wanted him so badly right then. I wanted to feel him fill me with his cock and hold me down with his weight as we came together. He wasn't ready yet, though, and he lowered his lips to my breasts first.

Each kiss of his lips to my skin was a slow, reverent, moist caress, moving with agonizing slowness over my body. With each kiss, my body turned hotter, my skin prickling in anticipation of his next kiss. My nipples puckered and stiffened as he pinched one and licked the other. I was dripping from between my thighs, wanting, needing to feel his mouth move there next, but he didn't, even when he kissed his way down my belly to my pubis and hip bones. I spread my legs apart, willing him to put his tongue inside me, but he licked my inner thigh instead, just outside my labia, then across my belly and down the other thigh.

I tugged a pillow from the head of the bed and stuck it under my back, elevating my hips to make it easier for him. He kissed my calf and behind my knees instead, then the soles of my feet. He ran his hands up my legs ahead of his kisses, touching his lips to my quad muscles, and then my hip bones again, and finally, at last, to my pussy. It was a kiss, at first, just his lips stroking my entrance, then a single shallow lap of his tongue.

Oh, lord, I thought, *he's really drawing this out*. His slow and methodical pace, his mouth and hands' detailed attention to every inch of my body brought my desire to furious life, making me desperate for him to lick me, to be hard and ready to push into me, fill me with his cock.

He refused to rush, though, and when he at long last dipped his tongue against my clit, I moaned out loud and pulled his head shamelessly against me. He rewarded me with a swift circle of my clit and a finger striking into me, curling in to stroke my walls and find my G-spot. After one swift circle, he resumed his unhurried bottom-to-top licks, focusing the apex of each swipe on my aching nub.

I'd come already, and hard, and I was anticipating another body-shivering explosion.

I wasn't disappointed.

He never increased his pace, even when he had to know by my breathing and moaning and desperate undulation of my hips that I was close. He paused once to spit into his hand, smearing the saliva against my asshole. His other finger was deep inside my pussy and stroking slowly, his tongue gliding in lazy circles around my clit.

He touched a finger to my tightest hole, paused, and looked at me for approval.

"Do it," I breathed. "Gently."

He didn't answer, just pushed his finger against me, not trying to shove in but to coax the opening to stretch. His tongue and other finger had slowed to almost stillness, but not quite. And then he was inside, just his pinky finger. I gasped and drew my knees up, trying to relax the muscles. He left his finger there, letting me acclimatize to his presence, and then moved deeper with his characteristic gentle, unhurried pace.

His tongue began to move again, flicking my clit, and his finger moved in my pussy to stroke the rough patch of my G-spot, and now the fire and pressure began to burgeon. My breathing was a long-drawn, high-pitched moan, rising into a panting whimper as the climax rose to frenzied peak, his pinky working its way ever deeper until I felt his knuckles against me. I clawed my fingers into the bed and didn't even try to dampen my scream of climax, feeling ecstatic detonations rip through me. My pussy clenched around his fingers and my asshole clamped around his pinky and he was moving both hands in tandem, his pinky more slowly and shallowly, and I was blind and deaf and mute, every muscle, every fiber, every synapse of my being on fire and in twisting paroxysms of delight, and he did not relent.

When finally he removed his fingers from me, I went limp, shuddering with ripples of pleasure.

Jeff brushed his lips against my ear and whispered, "I'll be right back."

I couldn't have moved if I wanted to, and right then, all I wanted was to stay still and bask in the glow of a glorious orgasm.

He came back, put his hand in mine, and helped me sit up. "Come on," he said to me, pulling me to my feet.

"Where are we going?"

"You'll see." He nipped my throat with a kiss and led me to his living room and out onto his back porch.

I hesitated on the threshold of the door-wall. "Outside? But...I'm naked."

"So am I," Jeff said. "There's a privacy fence, for one thing, and I only have neighbors on one side, for another, and for a third, I've got a wall around the hot tub."

I let him pull me outside, and sure enough, he had a ten-foot-tall fence between his backyard and the neighbors. In addition to the privacy fence, he had built a three-sided wall around the hot tub.

The night was pitch black, and the tub glowed

with wavering, submerged yellow light. A small, round three-legged table stood to one side, a massive, four-wick white candle flickering merrily, and a bottle of wine. It was a small touch, just a table, a candle, and a bottle, but it was enough to show he'd made an effort. It wasn't just sex for Jeff.

Oh, shit. The thought was a flash through my head, but enough to make me wonder what I'd gotten myself into. And then Jeff's arms were around my bare waist and pulling me into a breath-defying kiss and all thoughts and worries were gone.

We broke apart long enough to step into the hot tub. It was scalding, and I wasn't ready to sink down into it yet. I held on to Jeff, one arm around his neck, the other toying with his cock, testing his readiness for round two. Oh, he was ready.

He grew rigid under my hand, standing upright, unfolding, uncoiling. I put one foot up on the side of the tub and lifted up onto my toes, a gush of wetness spreading through me in eager hunger to feel him spear into me, fill me past full. Jeff rumbled deep in his chest as he probed my pussy with his tip. I sank down from my tiptoes, plunging him up into me. He spread me apart, pushing in and rising up on his toes until he was hilt-deep.

He sat down, easing us into the water. I put my legs on either side of his hips and he braced himself with his feet on the far edge of the tub, his hands supporting his weight and mine on the seats.

Holy shit, he's strong, I thought. He held us without straining, both of our bodies' weight held by the power of his arms and core. I sought the tub bottom with my toes, but he held me aloft, smirking he as began to thrust.

"Jeff, you're crazy," I gasped, laughing.

I was waist deep in the water, and he let us sink down, floating nearly weightless, and then he powered upward, spearing deep and then relaxing, only to thrust again. I curled over him, mouth quivering, breathless, as he moved. I was near climax almost instantly, burning all over again, boiling with pressure.

He sank to a sitting position on the bottom, and I wrapped my legs around his waist, the water at his chin and at my throat. He tilted his head up and I pressed my lips to his, tasting the tang of my essence on his tongue. He rolled his hips into mine, barely moving inside me, just enough to keep the pressure building.

The wine was open, and I reached for the bottle, tilted it to my lips, and drank. It was a sweet red, inexpensive but delicious.

"I forgot glasses, didn't I?" Jeff said, taking the bottle from me.

"It's fine," I answered. "I'm not above drinking from the bottle."

We took turns drinking straight from the bottle, our hips rolling in synch all the while, until my climax was nearing peak, until I couldn't hold the bottle, so unsteady were my hands. The water was hot, the air with a bite of near-fall cool, and the night silent but for our breathing and the gentle bubble of the water.

Jeff set the half-empty bottle down and took my waist in his hands, lifting me and pulling me down in an increasing rhythm. I bowed my back and bit his shoulder as the fire began to spread, turning from a slow blaze into a wild inferno, heat spreading through me until my hair stuck in damp tendrils to my forehead and cheeks, until I was sure the boiling of the water around us was due to the heat radiating out of me.

Jeff began to groan, lifting and pulling me, thrusting upward, never letting our hips part, driving himself deep, and then his groans turned into my name, "*Ann*a, *Ann*a, *Ann*a," pulsing deeper into me with each syllable. He pressed his lips to my throat and began to thrust harder, splashing water now, his arms curled up around my shoulders and dragging me down, down, down, harder, harder, harder, and I came, came so hard stars burst behind my eyes and my fingers gouged into his back and my face tipped up to gasp whimpering gusts of air into my heaving lungs.

He came, then, exploding into me, thrusting upward so hard I had to fall forward and clutch myself to his hot, dripping chest and cling to him as he lifted me clear of the water, the wet heat of his seed crashing against my inner walls in an endless flood.

"Oh, my lord...oh, my Anna," Jeff whispered, sinking down and stroking my hair from my face.

"God, that was intense," I breathed, nestled against his chest, his cock still buried inside me.

"I don't want to leave you," he said. "I mean, I want to stay inside you."

I wiggled my hips down onto him. "So don't. Let's stay like this until you're hard, and then we can do it all over again."

He reached for the wine and we drank, me still sitting on his lap, the water bubbling around us, flushing us with heat.

I've never been a make-out-session kind of girl. I like kissing all right, but as a means to an end. When I kiss a man, it gets my juices flowing and all I want to do is keep going, not just kiss all night.

Then Jeff kissed me, post-coital, in the hot tub, and all that changed. It was a slow, delicate kiss, moving and shifting in its own rhythm, drawing me into it, pulling me down into the substance of the moment. For the first time in my life, I lost myself in a kiss, drowned in the taste of the man, the feel of his body around me, his strength supporting me, his manhood slick inside my sex.

It was just a kiss at first, and it continued thus for a timeless eternity, minutes and hours passing out of awareness, until I wasn't sure which way was up, where I was or even who I was, outside of the roaring passion of our lips' and bodies' matched fervor.

And then, gradually, he grew within me, hardening and lengthening, almost imperceptibly at first, but more noticeably with every passing second. His hands lifted to find my breasts, and with that sensual touch my awareness of sensation beyond the kiss broadened to include his cock inside me and his hips beginning to move and my pussy beginning to glide on him then...

The world was obliterated. There was nothing but orgasmic brilliance, instant ecstasy from the very first full thrust, lasting for a time without time as he crushed into me, and I came again and again, until I was limp on top of him and still coming, shudders rocking through me with each roll of his hips, so much unending climactic fury that I couldn't contain it, could only writhe helpless on top of him until he began to grunt, moving in a thrashing rhythm into me, his breathing in my ear almost panicked; when he came, I fell over the edge of sanity into something else, and he clutched me as if he too had passed beyond the ability to contain the spreading infinity coursing between and in and through us.

Jeff had a way of making even a night spent in his living room seem exciting and fun.

One night, our DJ shift ended early, since the bar hadn't seen a single customer—other than Earl, the old graybeard in a John Deere cap who drank there every night—in more than two hours. We packed up, got takeout Chinese, a six-pack of cupcakes, a couple bottles of wine, and went back to Jeff's house.

We ate on the couch, watched *Bones*, and got drunk. This may not sound like fun, but it was. Well, maybe not fun, like bowling or go-karts or kinky sex, but it was satisfying. Pleasant.

After we threw away the leftovers and Styrofoam and those stupid square white boxes, Jeff pushed me down onto the couch, refilled my wine, and then shot me a mischievous smirk. I sipped my wine and waited. Jeff scooped up the remote and changed the channel to *Bravo*. Apparently he knew my dirty little secret: an addiction to *Real Housewives*. I'd never tried to make him watch it with me, figuring no self-respecting guy would like it. New Jersey was on, my personal favorite.

He still had the silly grin on his face, letting me know he wasn't done. I wasn't sure how much better it could get, though. I mean, *Real Housewives of New Jersey* and wine?

It got better. He unwrapped a bumpy cake cupcake, handed it to me, and then knelt down in front of me.

"What are you doing?" I finally asked.

"You'll see. Just sit back and watch your show. Pay no attention to me."

He had something up his sleeve, I just knew it. He waited until I was immersed in my show, then rested his hands on my knees. I glanced at him, but he only shrugged and grinned.

"You're being weird, Jeff."

"No I'm not, I'm just drunk." Jeff laughed. "Now sit back."

I sat back, confused but curious.

Jeff's hands slid up my thighs to cup the curved sides of my ass, then arced across to unbutton my pants with a swift, feather-light touch.

"What are you doing?" I demanded.

"Nothing," Jeff said, unzipping my pants and tugging them down.

I lifted my ass up and with a single tug the jeans and panties were off.

"This doesn't seem like nothing," I said.

Jeff just smiled and touched his stubbled mouth to my knee, then the soft, sensitive skin of my inner thigh.

"Want me to stop?" Jeff asked, his lips nearly to my crotch now, moving to the other leg and tickling my flesh with hot, wet kisses.

I opened my mouth to answer, but my breath was stolen by his lips grazing my mound, his tongue laving over my labia. My hands were occupied, holding a wine glass in one hand and a cupcake in the other, and I realized this was his plan all along. He knew my favorite things, and was giving them to me all at once.

I closed my eyes and shut out Theresa's shrill voice, sipped my wine as Jeff's tongue speared into me. The wine burned hot and dry as it slipped down my throat, and Jeff's tongue licked waves of heat and moist desire through my nether lips. I took another sip and followed it with a taste of icing as he slipped two fingers between my swollen labia and inside me, curling up to stroke the hypersensitive patch of skin high inside my walls.

This was sensation overload. The icing was sweet, the chocolate rich and crumbling, the wine potent and robust, and Jeff's fingers and tongue licked and swiped and swirled. Waves of rising climax sliced through me, fire and spasm and pressure all at once.

In the background, Caroline and Jacqueline and Theresa argued in overlapping voices, and I only heard every third word, the familiar themes of their recurring issues washing over me.

Jeff's unoccupied hand traced up my belly and under my shirt, tugged the cups of my bra down to free my nipples, and now his fingers rolled the taut responsive nubs, pushing the volcanic pressure of pending orgasm higher and higher. I gasped and bucked my hips as he increased his pace, his tongue circling my clit in narrowing concentric rings, his fingers on my G-spot and my nipple matching the rhythm, and I was on the edge, about to explode, god, so close, and then...he slowed nearly to a stop. I wanted to scream, opened my mouth to say something in protest, but he abruptly resumed his frenzied rhythm and I was barreling toward the edge once more.

At exactly the moment I was about to reach climax, Jeff slowed once more. When I took a breath to speak, Jeff pushed the wine toward my mouth, and I took another dutiful sip, feeling my head spinning from the wine, my palate exploding with the contradicting tastes of dry red wine and rich chocolate and sweet white icing.

Once more Jeff's tongue swiped in quick circles, his fingers stroking in time with his tongue, my nipples pinched and rolled and flicked, and now I was near the edge again.

"Let me come, Jeff," I gasped. "I'm so close, please...oh, god, yes..."

He matched the rocking of my hips, driving his long, quick tongue into me, and as I whispered his name he swept his tongue directly across my clit, striking the stiffened bundle of aroused nerves with the tip of his tongue. At the same moment, he pinched my nipple hard, stroked my G-spot with one finger, and I came in a blinding rush. Every nerve was ending on fire, my body exploding, my breathing caught and stopped. My spine arched into a bow shape, wine sloshed over my thumb, and Jeff continued spearing his tongue into my clit, pushing my orgasm higher, the pent-up pressure billowing through me in a flood of ecstasy.

When the fires cooled and Jeff rolled back onto his butt, I could only sit limp and gasp for breath as aftershocks rocked through me. I felt Jeff's tongue lap at my hand where the wine had spilled.

"You crushed the cupcake," Jeff said with an amused chuckle.

I opened my eyes and glanced at my hand. When I came, my fist had clenched involuntarily, and now chocolate crumbs were spilling over my hand. Jeff just laughed and took the remainder from me, threw it away, and sucked up the crumbs with a hand vacuum before sitting down next to me with a glass of wine.

"That was incredible," I said.

"You liked it?"

I laughed. "I'm not sure how it could have gotten any better," I said.

"Then my work here is done," Jeff said, a satisfied grin on his face.

I noted a telltale bulge against the zipper of his jeans. I knew Jeff well enough to know he wouldn't ask for a return favor. He wasn't looking at me as he carefully and methodically devoured a bumpy cake. I was struck by an idea.

I slipped off the couch and knelt between his

knees. Jeff just quirked an eyebrow and took a slow, deliberate bite, and then washed it down as I unbuttoned his pants. I unzipped him and pulled the jeans and boxers off, then took a cupcake from the plastic container. Jeff seemed less sure of what I was doing, suddenly. I broke the hardened chocolate shell of the bumpy cake to get at the icing beneath.

Wrapping one hand around the base of Jeff's cock, I dipped the fingers of my other hand into the icing. I smeared it over the tip of his shaft, dipped into the icing again, and spread it down the length of him.

"Icing has always been my favorite part of a cupcake," I said.

Jeff grinned, then hissed as I licked up his cock from the root to the tip. His head flopped back against the couch as I swiped my tongue along his icing-covered flesh again, licking him as if his cock was an ice cream cone. I cupped his balls in one hand and gently massaged them as I wrapped my lips around his tip, took him into my mouth, backed away, and then bobbed down again. He gasped as I moved my fist up and down his length, sucking on his engorged, icing-smeared head. My saliva and the icing became a slick lubricant, and my fist slipped on his length without friction, and now I was sucking hard enough to hollow my cheeks. He arched his back, stuttered a garbled warning just before he jerked his hips and came. I continued to move my fingers and mouth on him as he came, drawing the seed from him until he was softening in my hand.

Jeff looked at me with heavy-lidded eyes, a hazy smile on his face. I went to the kitchen, wet a paper towel, and cleaned him carefully. I didn't imagine it would be fun to be sticky, after all.

We sat, half-naked, and finished our wine, and Jeff actually watched the show with me, although he muttered, "they're all fucking nuts," every five minutes the entire time.

I knew one thing for sure: I'd never look at cupcakes the same way after that night.

A little over two weeks passed, and Jeff and I spent almost every spare moment that we could together, working, sleeping, eating, and making love...having sex...fucking. I wasn't sure what to call it, what word to use.

Nothing we did was wild or kinky, just vanilla, multi-positional sex, but he rocked my world every single time. He was unfailingly slow in all things, never rushing to take me, never moving into me until I had found climax at least once, never allowing me to come down from climax until I was limp as a dishrag and completely sated.

He was wonderful. He was attentive. He was polite and considerate, and incredible in bed, and...

I panicked.

The panic began with an envelope with a New York, New York, return address, and the one name that could throw me for a loop: Chase Delany. Eleven letters, and I was sweating, my heart hammering, confusion pumping through me, and I hadn't even opened it yet.

Jeff had swung me by my apartment so I could get clothes and check my mail and appease Jaime for having vanished for two weeks. I sorted through the mail: *bill, bill, junk, bill...holy shit what is this?*

Jeff noticed me freeze with the envelope in my hands.

"What is it?" he asked, concern tingeing his voice.

"A letter." My voice was small and tight.

"From?"

A pause too long. "Chase."

An even longer pause. "Chase." A lift of the chest and a slow outbreath was his only reaction. "Might as well open it, then." Jeff's eyes were shuttered, cold, and guarded.

I opened the letter. A plane ticket to New York fell out of the envelope, and I unfolded the letter with trembling fingers:

> *I need to see you.*
> —*Chase*

I tossed the letter on my lap and sighed, a long, shuddering, almost-but-not-quite-crying whimper of desperate confusion. My thoughts were a jumble of noise and curses and hysteria.

What do I do? What do I do?

The thought repeated itself, over and over. Jeff kept silent and drove. I thought of Chase, of the one night I'd had with him. He made me feel alive as never before. He'd awakened my hunger not just for sex but for life. I would never have even considered being with Jeff if it wasn't for my time with Chase.

And god, Chase had done things to me that I didn't know were possible. He'd done hot, kind of kinky things that I really had liked, and wanted again. And again.

Jeff...god, the man didn't need any of that to rock my existence.

But Jeff wanted more. Expected more. Needed and deserved more. It wasn't just sex for Jeff. And I wasn't sure I wanted that, at least not yet.

Jeff finally pulled his Yukon over to the side of the road. We were on a dirt road in the middle of nowhere, fields on both sides, a glowering gray sky heavy around us and threatening rain, trees in the distance. AM talk radio whispered in the background, only audible in the silence as Jeff waited for me to speak. He wouldn't ask. If I didn't say anything, he'd just wait until it was clear I wasn't talking, and that would be that.

"He...he wants me to visit him in New York."

The words were like small, hard stones tumbling out of my mouth.

A long, fraught silence. "And you want to go."

"I don't know, Jeff. I don't know." I picked up the plane ticket and stared at it like it could answer my dilemma. "Yes, I do. But I also don't."

Silence, Jeff staring out the window as raindrops plopped in slow, staccato rhythm on the windshield, abruptly blossoming into a downpour.

"Say something," I said.

"So go. Don't let me hold you back. If New York is where you want to be, then go. Be happy. We had fun while it lasted." His voice was a study of nonchalance.

"Jeff, I—"

"It's fine, Anna." Jeff pulled the gearshift into drive, slowly and carefully, as if he wanted to slam it but wouldn't let himself. "You do want to go. I can see it in your face, but you're worried about hurting me. Don't. I'll be fine."

He made a U-turn and took me home, driving in silence. When we pulled back into the parking lot of my apartment complex, he put it in park and finally met my eyes.

"Be happy, Anna. If that means going to New York to be with Chase, then go."

"Jeff?"

He cut me off with a kiss—slow, as all things with Jeff are—and delicate. A farewell.

"Goodbye, Anna." It was a dismissal.

I got out of the vehicle and went to my door. Jeff pulled out backward and drove away without looking at me.

My flight was for ten the next morning.

I was on it.

Big Girls Do It Wilder

ONE GLIMPSE OF CHASE DELANY in leather pants, a tight T-shirt, and shit-kicker boots was all it took to get my libido raging, and to drive away any lingering doubts about coming to New York.

Well, the doubts were still there; they were just pushed down under a torrent of lust.

He stood waiting for me, thick arms crossed over his broad chest, dark hair messy and sort-of-but-not-quite spiked, brown eyes blazing. He looked like he could, and would, drag me to the nearest bathroom and fuck me in a toilet stall. How do you resist that kind of naked lust?

You don't.

He pulled me into a hug, palms circling on my back, drifting lower and lower, and then he grabbed my ass in full view of everyone in the airport. I opened my mouth to protest, and then he kissed me, hard enough to take my breath away and make me forget what I was saying.

I'd almost forgotten how he could do that.

"Come on, hot stuff," he said, "I've got a cab waiting."

He pulled me into a fast walk, and I forgot to ream him out for groping me in public. *Besides*, I asked myself, *how much do I really mind? Not so much*, came the answer. He was claiming me. I didn't mind being claimed. And oh, boy, the promise of the things he would do with his hands, when we were in private, had my blood racing.

"How was the flight?" he asked.

"Fine. Nothing eventful. How's things with the band coming?"

"Great! We're in the studio right now, recording our first single. Once that's in post, we're going on tour, just local stuff at first, New York, Buffalo, Atlantic City, DC. We'll be opening for some big-name bands, though, so it'll be great exposure." He squeezed my hand, his excitement palpable, radiating off him in waves. "Have you ever been to a recording studio? I'll bring you with me. You'll love it. It's so fun."

He chattered all the way through baggage claim and out to the taxi line. The taxi ride into the city was full of more Chase-chatter with barely a pause for breath. He didn't ask me much of anything about how I'd been since I'd seen him last.

His hand crept up my leg as we sat in the back of the taxi, and slowly crawled up to the hem of my skirt. I let his chatter wash over me and focused on wondering how far his hand would venture, and how far I'd let it. The cabbie's eyes flicked back to us every once in a while, and I wondered how much he could see through the rearview mirror. I tried to think about being in a car, driving, looking in the mirror into the back seat.

You can't see much, can you?

I smirked, and decided to let Chase explore as far as he wanted, just as a dare. I let my legs loosen a little, and Chase's fingers made their first exploratory move under the hem. It wasn't much of a skirt, really. Short enough to need my legs crossed when sitting in view of others.

Chase was going on about isolating the instruments and layering them in post-production, and how his bassist had trouble playing his part without the rest of the band. I nodded, made agreeable noises at the appropriate places, and slid my bottom down a bit farther.

His fingers were tickling my inner thighs, working upward. Another shift of my legs, and his forefinger was brushing my pussy through the thin silk of my panties. I bit my tongue and forced myself to keep still. He glanced at me and grinned, a cat's-caught-the-canary smile. Then his middle finger worked its way underneath the band next to my leg to slip into my folds, which grew wetter the farther he got.

He never slowed his patter as he found my clit with one finger, and now he circled it, slow and soft. I swallowed hard and tried not to gasp when the climax began almost immediately. God, was I ready. It was as much anticipation as anything. The memory of what Chase could do, and would do.

A soft sigh escaped me, and the cabbie glanced back, a smile crinkling the corners of his eyes. *He knows*, I thought. But I didn't care. I was close, raging and ready. He never increased his pace, just kept a slow and steady stroking rhythm, even when the cabbie struck up a conversation about...I don't even know what. Something inane. My thoughts were a jumbled mess, scattered and lost in the blaze of a rising climax that wouldn't pass the edge.

I put my hand over his and pushed, wanting him to go faster, harder, but he only let a corner of his mouth tip up in a mocking smirk.

The bastard is playing with me, I realized.

By the time the cabbie let us out at Chase's address, a modest walk-up shared with the rest of the band, I was a quivering, knock-kneed wreck. Chase grabbed my single suitcase from the trunk, paid the driver, and led me in. He gave me a tour, a long, detailed tour. He introduced me to his friends/band-mates/roommates, and made sure they engaged me in witty banter. Witty fucking banter, when I was a few good touches away from coming, and hard.

I was on the edge still, every step brushing my thighs together and making my nub ache harder. It didn't help that Chase took every opportunity during the tour and the conversation to touch me in some surreptitious way, just enough to keep my desire alive and burning.

I was snarling with unfulfilled sexual need and irritation by the time Chase showed me to his room and closed the door behind him, twisting the lock with a flourish. He held my bag in one hand, the other in his pocket, a shit-eating grin on his face. I was flushed, my hair sticking to my temples, my legs shaking like leaves.

"Miss me?" Chase asked. Cocky bastard.

I attacked him. I mean, I just about flying tackled him. He dropped the suitcase with a loud thud and caught me against his chest, our tongues clashing and colliding, hands ripping zippers open and peeling clothes off.

Chase pushed me away, chest heaving, and pulled my shirt over my head, going slowly now, and then pushed my skirt down past my hips. He was hard, his erection bulging against his pants, and I reached for him, but he moved out of reach.

"My turn first," he said, unhooking my bra. "I've missed you. I need to see you."

I wasn't sure if that was a self-centered thing, or a compliment. It didn't matter. He had me naked in front of him, and he was running his hands over my body as if it were the most precious thing he'd ever seen and he simply couldn't get enough.

I was wet and trembling, aching. I wanted him to push me down onto the bed and slip inside me, take me hard, or slow, or anything.

"Take me, Chase," I breathed. "Take me, please."

"Are you begging me?" Chase asked, rolling a nipple gently between a thumb and forefinger.

I arched my back, thrusting my breast into his hand, and writhed my hips into his thigh.

"Yes." I wasn't above begging. "Please, Chase. I want you."

Chase stepped back, taking his hands off me. "Say it, baby. Beg me."

He wanted me to play the game. Well, I could play, too. He was hard, and I knew he wanted me. His eyes betrayed him. The twitching curl of his fingers betrayed him.

I moved toward him, putting an extravagant sway to my hips. I slipped my hands underneath his shirt to his nipples and pinched, hard. He grimaced and tried to escape, but I followed him. I bit his earlobe, breathing into his ear, and dug a single finger under the waistband of his leather pants, brushing the tip of his cock. His stomach jerked inward, and his hands flew to my waist, then down and cupped my ass, pulled me against him. I circled around behind him, kissing his neck, his jaw, and his ear again.

"Beg you?" I whispered. "How about you beg me?"

Chase squared his shoulders and set his jaw. "I don't think so."

I laughed, and reached around his waist to unbutton his pants. His hands groped behind to reach for me, but all he could reach at this angle were my hips. I let him touch me. My hips ground into his ass, and I tugged his pants down, just enough to free the tip of his cock.

"I'm so wet, Chase," I whispered, rubbing the pad of my thumb on the drop of pre-come oozing from him. "I'm wet for you. I'm aching. I want you inside me. I want you to fuck me, Chase."

He tried to turn around, but I danced to follow his motion, and he went still. "It's not nice to tease a girl. Don't you know that?" I said. Chase groaned.

I dipped my hand into his boxer-briefs to take his full length in one hand. He rolled his hips, but I let go, scraping the tip with a fingernail in slow, gentle circles.

"How about you beg me," I whispered. "You know I want you. I could drop to my knees and suck you off, right now. All you have to do is beg."

Chase sucked in his breath between his teeth, but otherwise kept silent and still. I pushed his pants down a bit farther, past his hips. My teeth at his earlobe again, I took his balls in one hand and his cock in the other, stroking and massaging. Chase refused to move, even when I began pumping him. A change in tactics was required, then. I pulled his shirt off with one hand, still sliding my fist up and down his length. He couldn't stop his breathing from changing, though, and I knew he was nearing the end of his control.

Next came the pants, which were more of a struggle with one hand, but I did it, along with some judicious use of my feet. He was naked too, then, and my hands were doing their slow work on his cock, his breathing growing ragged, his hips beginning to tremble despite his attempts at control. At last, a moan escaped his lips, and that was my cue.

I let go of his shaft and massaged his sack, pressing a finger in a gentle circle to his taint. He groaned, growled, and thrust his hips, close, so close, but unable to come without me. He grabbed for my hands, but I resisted his attempts to guide me back to him.

"Anna," he said, his voice ragged. "Goddamn it."

I moved in front of him, pressed my body against his, slid my pussy against him, ground into him, slipped my hands over his body, kissed him everywhere.

Time for the real teasing.

I dropped to my knees, kissing his torso on the way down, took him in my hands again, caressed his cock in a hand-over-hand motion. He threw his head back, anticipating.

Anticipate away, baby, I thought. *Not gonna happen how you think it is.*

I even went so far as to wrap my lips around his head and suck until my cheeks hollowed. He was close; I could feel him tensing, about to come, and I spat him out again, glancing up at him, a wicked smile on my face.

"Oh, I'm sorry, were you about to come?" I said, trying to sound innocent.

Chase growled at me and tangled his fingers in my hair, but didn't apply any pressure.

"Not gonna work," he growled.

I lifted an eyebrow in a "we'll see" gesture. I took him in my mouth again, stroking him with my hands now as I bobbed on him, put a finger to his taint again and massaged, faster now, hands sliding up and down, lips sealed around his head, and his knees began to move....

This time his growl of frustration was loud and irritated.

I crawled onto the bed, lay on my back, and spread my knees wide. Chase's eyes followed me, hungry and predatory. I slid my hands on my skin, rubbing up from my belly to take my breasts in my hands, thumbing the nipples, hefting the heavy mounds, then down between my legs. Slow, then. A single finger tracing the crease between my labia, dipping in to swipe the slick juices.

"Look how wet I am," I said, showing my glistening finger. "You want me?"

Chase crawled up on the bed, eyes burning. I slapped my knees closed and covered my breasts with my arms, as if suddenly demure.

"Tell me you want me," I said.

Chase rocked back on his knees, brow furrowed in irritation. "You know I do."

"Say it."

"I want you."

I shook my head. "Tell me what you want to do to me."

"I want to tie you up and fuck you until you can't walk."

I widened my eyes as if shocked. Chase grinned and scooted off the bed, rummaged in a dresser drawer, and pulled out four neckties. He held them up, two in each hand.

I spread my hands and feet wide, waiting for him. This time, he tied my hands and feet both, and I felt a rush of true nerves then. With my feet free, I wasn't as vulnerable. I was completely at his mercy.

I was spread-eagled before him, and now he climbed up on the bed between my legs, ran his hands up from my knees to my thighs, dragged a thumb down my pussy, not entering, but teasing.

He could tease me as long as he wanted, touch me until I was near to orgasm and then stop. For hours, if he wanted. I refused to let fear show on my face. I squeezed my eyes shut and pretended indifference as he teased my entrance with a finger.

A single push inside, one finger. I gasped, bucked my hips. I kept my eyes closed, enjoying the sensation without sight. Two fingers then, curling up to caress my G-spot, and now I whimpered. Two fingers and a tongue, stroking my walls and licking my clit, and I jerked my hands against the bonds holding me in place.

Climax rising, rising, fire burning, and Chase kept going, bringing me to the edge.

"Don't stop, please, please don't stop," I said.

He didn't stop. He flicked and stroked and licked me over the precipice, and I moaned, refusing to scream. He didn't stop, though. I was hypersensitive, every touch like fire on my skin, and I wanted him to stop, to give me a minute, but he didn't. This was a new torture. He withdrew his fingers and used his tongue alone, moving in circles and squares, side to side and up and down, and now...holy shit, another orgasm blossomed through me and I bit off a shriek of ecstasy, pleasure so potent it was like pain.

His weight descended on me, and now I felt a new pressure probing my entrance, his cock now, finally. But he didn't enter me. Oh, how I wanted to beg him, but refused. He pushed the very tip inside, gripped himself in his hand, and moved his cock in circles inside me, brushing my clit, and now it was there, his moist tip against my throbbing nub. He thrust, ever so slightly, sex in miniature. I sucked in a ragged breath at the flush of lightning bursting through me.

And then he pulled away, probably about to come himself. His lips found my breast, and his fingers the other, and now I entered a new realm of heaven as he licked and laved and tongued and pinched me.

There was no warning. He thrust inside me in one push, driving to the hilt, hard. My eyes flew open and I breathed a whimper, straining against the ties. His mouth remained on my nipple, and he didn't thrust again, just stayed there, buried to the root, our hips grinding together. I tried to move into him, but he held my hips down with one hand.

He was inside me, and another climax was building. I wanted him to move, needed him to thrust.

"Please…" I couldn't help myself.

He didn't move. He grazed his teeth on my stiffened nipple, then moved to the other. His hand held me down, kept me from rolling my hips.

"Damn it, Chase, please!"

I was past games. I'd come twice without him inside me, and it just wasn't the same. I wanted him deep, wanted to feel his length sliding inside me.

"Please what?"

"Enough teasing. Just fuck me."

"Hard, or soft?" He accompanied his question with a slow pull out and a hard thrust in.

"God, yes, just like that. Both. Either. I don't care!"

He moved again like he had before, a torturously slow withdrawal, until only the very tip was left inside me, and he hesitated there, stopping the flutter of my hips with his powerful hand, and then he crashed back into me. I gasped when he plunged in. He did it again, and again, slow out, fast in.

Then he switched, pulling out quickly and driving in as slow as he could. More teasing. I wanted rhythm, I wanted him to move and move and move, hard and fast or slow and soft, I didn't care, but I couldn't find release like this. It felt delicious, but it wouldn't bring me over the edge.

He switched tactics again, now adjusting the depth of his strokes, shallow, shallow, setting a rhythm but only a few inches in and out.

Maddening. Deeper now, yes, I whispered encouragement, gasped his name as he neared what I wanted, deep thrusts hard inside me.

I felt him abandon the games. He settled his weight on me, forearms planted underneath my neck, his lips crushing mine in hungry kisses. Finally, thank god, he drew out and plunged in, deep, as far as he could go, and again, a slow rhythm at last.

"God, Anna. I missed you. I missed this, so much."

I'd missed it, too, but I couldn't speak to say it. The anticipation of this, all the many minutes of teasing, had me desperate for him, had the explosion wild and rampant through me, but I couldn't move anything by my hips in the shallowest of rolls. I wanted to wrap myself around him, hold him as he drove into me, faster now, but I couldn't.

I tugged at the ties, jerked my feet, bucked wildly as he moved above me.

"Oh, god, oh, god," I moaned, needing to be freed, "let me go, let me go!"

He was gone, lost in the frenzy, and I could only gasp his name. He came, hard, so hard, and the fiery liquid of his seed filling me sent me over the edge, the mad thrust of his cock inside me sent me over the edge, his body going stiff in the throes of orgasm sent me over the edge.

This climax made stars crash in blinding bursts behind my eyes, and I couldn't stop the shrieks this time. Fire in my veins, in my muscles, in every cell, but still he thrust, pushing me past orgasm into desperation, back into pleasure so powerful it hurt.

At long last his motion slowed, and he untied me with trembling fingers.

Something twinged in my heart, a brief but sharp pang of some emotion I didn't recognize. I didn't like it, didn't want to categorize it, and I pushed it away. I curled in to rest my head on Chase's chest.

"God, I needed that," Chase said, after a long silence.

"It was definitely intense," I said.

Chase gave me an odd look, which I interpreted to mean he'd expected me to say "me, too." Which was dangerously close to having to realize it hadn't actually been all that long...

Shit. This was awkward.

The look passed, and I let myself drowse, feeling Chase's arm around me, his thick pectoral muscle a perfect pillow.

I woke up to Chase shaking me gently.

"Come on, sleepyhead. We've got reservations."

"Hmmm-what?" I forced myself to a sitting position, the sheet pooling around my waist. "Reservations?"

"For dinner. This place my buddy knows about, real tiny, but really great food." He grinned and tugged the sheet off me. "So get moving. Dress up nice."

I'm not sure the restaurant even had a name, honestly. The menus were small squares of thick white paper printed in black calligraphy. There was no name, no prices, no descriptions, just the item name. Very...minimalist.

The food was delicious, though. Incredible, actually. Strange pairings like steak and roasted apple, or garlic hummus and pork chops with candied asparagus. Bizarre. I found myself having a really great time, which shouldn't have surprised me but did. I'd never been on a date with Chase. Never spoken to him outside of the Ram's Horn and our one night together.

I felt panic bloom in my chest as I thought about that. I didn't know Chase at all. I didn't know where he'd grown up, if he'd ever been married or engaged before, if his parents were alive or if he had siblings or if he liked vegetables.

What am I doing here? I shouldn't have come. This was stupid. I should have stayed in Detroit with—

I cut my train of thought off ruthlessly. I wouldn't, couldn't think about him while I was with Chase. That was too close to a whole mess of emotions I didn't want to think about.

"Anna?" Chase's voice cut through my tangle of thoughts.

"Hmm?"

"I asked if you'd ever been backstage before."

"You did?" I shook my head and tried to clear the thoughts away. "Sorry. I'm just...sorry. No, I haven't."

Chase frowned, then waved a hand in dismissal. "Anyway. I got a text while you were sleeping. Our agent booked us to play a club in Harlem tomorrow, opening for a local band. It's a great opportunity for the band, and I figured you could watch from backstage. It'll be fun."

"Sure, sounds great."

We finished eating in silence, and finally Chase set his fork down with a clatter. "You seem distracted."

"Sorry, Chase. Just...I was dealing with some drama back home when I got your letter."

"Anything you want to talk about?"

"No, not really," I said.

"Okay, well, I'm here if you do."

Throughout dessert—paper-thin crepes filled with handmade apricot preserves, dusted with powdered sugar—I learned Chase had an older brother in accounting, in Connecticut, and a younger sister studying law at Duke, parents both passed on, no grandparents, no uncles, no cousins. He'd been engaged once, three years ago, but it had ended due to her being a cheating skank.

I in turn told him about my sordid past, or some of it. I mentioned my mostly normal mom, including her predilection for popping Oxy like Tic Tacs, and I mentioned my brother, who'd joined the Marines out of high school and never came back. I didn't mention my dad, who'd been quick with the Jack Daniels and quicker with his fists. I also didn't mention the guy with the knife in the alley, my first time DJing when I was eighteen, before I met Jeff.

I suspected there were things he hadn't mentioned, and I didn't push.

I don't have to tell Jeff any of this, because he already knows. The thought was errant and unwelcome.

We left the restaurant and strolled down the street, Chase looking sexier than he had any right to in a different pair of leather pants, these faded, beaten gray, with a white button-down and a plain black tie loosely knotted around an open collar.

"How many pairs of leather pants do you have, exactly?" I asked.

Chase laughed. "Too many. They're my thing, you might say."

"Do you ever not wear leather pants?"

"Not if I can help it. They're suitable for all occasions. You can even wear them to weddings, if you pair them right."

I had to admit he did look sinfully sexy in leather pants, which reminded me of my nickname for him when I'd first met him: Mr. Sexypants.

Another errant thought flew through my head, a reminder of how long ago it seemed that I'd met Chase and had that night in his bed. By comparison, the weeks with Jeff had seemed endless, longer than they really had been. A lifetime, almost.

Why do I keep thinking about Jeff? I'm with Chase.

I threaded my arm around Chase's. "So, Mr. Sexypants. What's next?"

"Mr. Sexypants?" Chase quirked a corner of his lip up in an amused smile.

"That's the nickname I gave you the night we met."

"I can dig it." Chase tangled our fingers together. "Well, we can go have some drinks, or we can go back to my place and fuck like bunnies."

"Sounds good," I said.

"Which?"

"Both. Well, first the one, then the other."

Chase nodded, and we hailed a cab, ending up at a crowded bar stuffed with cheering sports fans and half-naked women. I felt overdressed in my miniskirt and halter top. I mean, seriously, most of the women I saw were wearing almost nothing, booty shorts halfway up their asses and a bra, if that. Chase's eyes wandered, as men's eyes will, but he soon turned his attention back to me. We drank vodka and cranberry juice and tried to talk over the noise. We were crushed into a back corner, standing up. I was up against the wall, Chase pressed into me, and we soon abandoned all pretense of conversation.

He focused on my neck for a while, his lips cold from his drink, his breath hot, and every kiss he planted in his slow descent to my breasts made my nipples stand higher and harder with desire. I couldn't help noticing we weren't the only couple thus occupied, as most of the dark corners were taken by couples in similar positions. A few seemed to be actually going at it, the girls on their date's laps.

His mouth finally found the edge of my shirt and could go no farther down, not without pulling my breast free, and hell no to that. Not in public. I didn't care how dark the corner was.

The problem was, I wanted it. He'd found my erect nipple even through the shirt and bra, scratching at it with a fingernail till it stood harder, and yes, his other hand slid up my skirt and stroked my damp panties. He was hard, his bulge against my belly, and I could almost but not quite make myself reach into his pants. No one was paying attention to anyone else, and any noises we might have made would have been swallowed by the too-loud music, the blare of the TVs, and the cheering, laughing, screaming, chattering buzz of the bar patrons.

My blood was racing, my heart hammering. He'd worked one finger around my panties, and I was lifting up on my toes as he worked it in slow circles.

Do it, Anna. No one's watching.

I dug my hand into his pants and touched him, felt sticky wetness smear my palm as I stroked him. He groaned against my chest, a sound felt in my bones rather than heard. I pulled his face up to mine and kissed him, heat blossoming in my belly as his tongue explored my lips.

A door opened not far away and a couple sneaked out, hand in hand, sated grins on their faces. I tugged Chase to the door I'd seen the other couple leave, discovered it to be a bathroom, of sorts. It clearly catered to this purpose, with a chaise lounge in one corner.

Chase grinned at me, then pushed me toward the lounge. I moved to lie back on it, but Chase had other ideas. He gripped my hips and turned me facing away from him. I knew what he wanted, and I went along with it. Shimmying my panties off and stuffing them in my purse, I knelt on the lounge chair on my hands and knees. Chase grinned and licked his lips, then pushed my skirt up over my hips.

He caressed my ass with a gentle hand, then smacked me, hard enough to make me shriek in surprise. More smooth circles on my ass cheek, then a smack. This time, he speared two fingers into my wet pussy at the same moment he smacked me, and I had to grip the arm of the lounge with one hand.

The bathroom door didn't have a lock. I realized this as Chase straddled the lounge chair standing up, positioning himself behind me. Anyone could walk in and see me getting railed from behind. It shouldn't have made me wetter, but it did.

A zipping sound, and then his fingers were replaced by his cock, and I bowed my back upward as he thrust into me. His hands gripped my hips and jerked me into him. He wasn't gentle, and I liked it. Oh, god, did I like it. He pounded into me, one hand on my hip, the other fingering my clit as he plunged. I didn't bother trying to muffle my moans as he drove into me, harder with each thrust, flesh slapping.

"God, you're so tight," Chase groaned. "I love fucking you like this."

"In...a public...bathroom?" I had to gasp the words past the grunt that escaped me at each thrust.

"It's hot, but no. I meant from behind."

I heard the door unlatch, and then a surprised male voice: "Whoa. Nice."

"Fuck off," Chase growled, and the door closed again.

I should have been mortified, but wasn't. I'd had more than a few vodka cranberries, and the shame was a low burn in the back of my head that I knew I'd feel later. But now, oh, god, now I didn't care, not with climax so close, not with Chase's cock slamming into me, and his finger working my clit as he thrust, adding an edge to the fire exploding through me, and the knowledge that someone else had seen me like this only fueled the fire, added a frenzy to it, and now I was falling over the edge.

"Give it to me," I groaned, "yes, give it to me."

"Say my name," Chase said. "Say my name."

"Chase, Chase." I breathed it.

Then he pushed a finger onto my asshole, not pushing in un-lubricated, thankfully, just circling, and I screamed into the arm of the lounge, my head thumping against the fabric as he pistoned his hips into me.

He came, then, slowing his thrusts but driving deeper than ever and his fingers dug into my skin and he froze with his hips to my ass, deep and spurting seed through me.

"God, Anna. You make me come so hard." He spoke slumped over me, breathing in stuttering gasps.

We cleaned up and left the bathroom, getting looks from more than one person, telling me we'd been heard as well as seen.

"Let's get out of here," I said to Chase.

Even my heady buzz couldn't cool the flaming of my cheeks.

"You don't want another drink?"

I stalked toward the door, trying to get away from the amused eyes I felt on me. "No. Not here at least."

"Honey, it's fine—"

Honey? I wondered where that endearment had come from.

"I want to go," I cut in.

"Okay, then."

We left and walked back to Chase's place in silence. I wasn't sure what I was feeling, and I didn't know how to express it.

"Anna, look, I—"

"I'm not mad. I've just never done anything like that before. They knew. They heard us."

"It wouldn't be the first time people have gotten carried away in that bathroom, I'd wager."

I gave him a cross look. "Well, it's the first time for me, and I don't know how to feel about it."

Chase pulled me to a stop at the bottom of his steps and held my arms. "Did you enjoy it?"

"Yeah. It was great. But—"

"Do you know any of them?"

"No, but—"

Chase stepped closer, and I could feel the heat radiating off him, his dark eyes burning into mine, intense and piercing. "Look. I've never been there

before, and neither have you. We didn't know anyone there, and we never will. Who cares if they
heard us? Who cares if someone saw us? They
were probably just jealous it wasn't them getting
hot and heavy in the bathroom."

"You've never been there before?" I was softening, and I realized I had been mad at him.

"No," Chase said. "I've heard about it from a
few different people, but I've never been there. I
didn't even know about the bathroom. That was
you."

"I saw a couple come out, and they'd obviously
just boned in there, so I figured…"

"It was hot. I've never had sex quite so publicly
before. It was kind of…"

"Exhilarating," I filled in.

We grinned at each other, and then we started
laughing.

"Whoa. Nice," Chase said, mimicking the
gravelly voice of the guy who'd walked in on us.

"He was talking about me," I said.

"Not arguing there," Chase said, smirking.
"Come on, let's go in. I have some Red Stripe."

A few more beers, and I found myself in Chase's
bed, pinned down by his weight and his hands on
my wrists as he slowly and thoroughly plundered
me. As I did every time, I came hard, and more
than once, before Chase finally fell asleep.

I lay awake for another hour or so, trying to sort through the jumble of emotions the day had engendered. "Trying" is the operative word, though. It was too tangled to figure out at three in the morning, half-drunk, and sexually exhausted.

We spent the next day on a tour of New York. Chase took me on the subway, in cabs and on foot, showed me the big tourists spots and then a few of the more underbelly sort of places. We had dinner at another tiny, out-of-the-way restaurant, and then it was time to get to the club where Six Feet Tall would perform. I helped set up, watched them warm up, and then the club started to fill up and Chase showed me a spot backstage.

Backstage turned out to be a busy place, bustling with techies, assistants, band members, and a host of other people whose functions I couldn't have even guessed at. Chase was in his element, wearing the sexiest pair of leather pants yet, ripped and tattered and weathered, knee-high boots with buckles and spikes and straps, and nothing else. His marvelous body was bare from the waist up, chiseled and cut, and even larger than ever, if that was possible. He'd rubbed oil into his muscles, and he had leather cuffs on his forearms that spanned from wrist to elbow, looking like something a medieval warrior would wear.

I couldn't take my eyes off him. He strode back and forth in the backstage area, clutching his mic in one hand, eyes bright and focused. His dark hair was wild, spiked, messy, as if he'd just fucked hard. Which he had. We'd found a bathroom, and Chase had backed me against a wall, lifted my leg around his hips and driven into me wildly until we both collapsed into each other. The sex had energized him, it seemed, made him buzz with psyched passion for his impending performance.

When the lights dimmed to black, he rounded on me, kissed me hard and fast.

"Kill 'em, baby," I said.

He grinned at me, then trotted out on stage with his band in tow.

Baby? Where the hell did that come from?

I shrugged it away as the lights came up with the drummer pounding a fast rhythm on the bass kick-drum. The bassist came in next, slapping his strings in a complicated riff, and then the guitarist wound in with a slippery, snaking tune. Chase stood bathed in a spotlight, hands at his sides, head down, motionless. I could pretty much hear all the women in the audience creaming themselves from this vision of him, huge and cut and dominating, even silent and still.

This was a rock band, no holds barred, just this side of metal, but with real melody and musicianship. The music continued, picking up pace and energy until it reached a crescendo, and then, on a single synchronized note, the band fell silent and Chase filled the space with his voice, a low vocalization that rose and rose and rose. The band kicked in, then, perfectly timed with the shift in his singing.

God, they were good. So good. The crowd went nuts, screaming, waving, suddenly pumped for a kick-ass opening number. His lyrics, oh, man. Deep, full of feeling and poetry. Intelligible and meaningful, unlike the tripe spouted by so many other bands these days. He meant every word.

And then, of course, after a few heavy-hitting numbers, the lights dimmed and the energy dropped. Chase sat with his legs dangling off the low stage, mic held in both hands, close to his face, eyes downcast as if seeing long-ago memories, and crooned a ridiculously touching ballad of heartbreak and loss and love. Of course, he sold it as dramatically as he did the angsty, angry numbers.

They finished their set, and I visited the bathroom while they loaded their gear. I found myself in a corner stall, sitting on the toilet and listening to a pair of girls primping at the mirror, discussing Chase.

"Ohmigod, is he hot or what?"

A second voice made a shrill squeal, and I could practically see her waving her face with her hands. "I mean, seriously. He's huge. I bet he's hung like a fucking horse."

The first girl popped her lips, reapplying lip-stick, probably, and then said, "Hung like a horse is right. You could totally see his package through his pants, and he wasn't even hard. I bet he's awesome in bed."

"I've heard he's into some weird shit. I know this chick who hooked up with him after a show once. She said he's hung like a fucking god, and that he's amazing in bed...if you like being tied up and spanked, among other things." A pause, then, "He can spank me as hard as he wants, I'd let him do anything. He can even put it in my ass."

"Marcia! That's nasty. And if he really is that huge, wouldn't it hurt?"

"Not if he's slow about putting it in. He's gotta work up to it, use his fingers first, and a lot of lube. It's really fucking hot, if he does it right."

"You've done anal?"

"Hell, yes. I let Doug fuck me in the ass all the time. It's hot. The fun part is, no condoms, and you can do it even during your period, if you're in the mood."

"God, that's so nasty. And I'm never in the mood when I'm on my period. I would never let Brian put it in my ass. He's asked a couple times, but I always say no. This ass is exit only."

"Well, mine isn't. That singer is so hot, he makes me wet just looking at him." A pause, hands being washed and dried. "I wonder if I can get backstage to meet him."

"I know one of the bouncers here. I'll get you backstage. I might even join you for a threesome with him. I'll bet he'd be down with that, if he's as kinky as Jenny said he was."

I was alone again, and I nearly vomited.

I found him by the stage, cornered by who I imagined were the girls from the bathroom. He hadn't seen me yet, so I stayed in the shadows, blatantly eavesdropping.

"So, do you have plans for later, Chase?"

"If you don't, we could grab a few drinks, maybe go by my place...hang out for a bit. You know, just see what pops up."

Chase looked awfully tempted. He actually hesitated. I saw him search the bar for me, and I sank back farther into the shadows by the hallway to the bathrooms.

"As much as I'd like to, ladies, I do have plans for tonight. Maybe another night, though. My next show is in a few days, and all the details are up on my band's website."

God. He knew exactly what they were proposing. I still felt ill. Why was I jealous?

I tried to shove it away. So what if he'd hooked up with someone before I got here. I had, hadn't I?

It wasn't just hooking up with Jeff, though. That meant something.

Shit. What did that mean? It meant something? Then why was I jealous of Chase? Why did the thought of him having a threesome with some groupie sluts bother me?

Because I could picture it easily. And I could see him honestly considering it, before realizing I was still here in New York with him and turning them down. But then he'd basically set up a rain check, hadn't he?

Maybe he didn't realize what they were getting at.

Yeah, right.

Where was I going to be in a few days? Here in New York still? The return flight was open-ended. We hadn't established a length of time for my visit. I'd told Jeff...well, I hadn't told him much of anything. He'd DJ without me.

Is Jeff hooking up with someone, now that I'm here in New York? That lovely thought made me sick, and I wanted to throw up yet again. Jealous of two men. Not good.

"Anna? Are you okay?" Chase's voice filtered through my fog of thoughts, and his hands gripped my arms.

"Sorry, yeah. I'm fine." I couldn't quite meet his eyes. If I did, I'd say something about the groupies from the bathroom, and that would complicate things. I didn't need more complication, or drama.

"You looked...I don't know...angry, or sick, or something. You sure you're okay?"

I forced a smile on my face. "Yeah, just... yeah. I'm fine." I made myself kiss him, knowing the groupies were watching from the bar; after a moment, I didn't need to make myself, because I was lost in the kiss. "Great show! You killed it! That ballad was wonderful."

"You liked it? I just wrote it the other day. That was the first time I've performed it live. I was so nervous I nearly harfed."

"It was incredible. You totally sold it."

"It was for you."

"It was about losing the love of your life." I gave him a confused look.

Chase grinned. "Well, I really wanted you to come with me."

"So you wrote a ballad about it?"

"Yep. I was heartbroken."

I crossed my arms under my breasts and gave him a skeptical eyebrow-raise. "Uh-huh. You're lucky you're cute, 'cause you're totally lying."

"Am not," Chase said, running his hands down my sides to my hips.

"Not cute, or not lying?"

"Not lying. I'm totally cute," he said.

"You sounded like a school girl just then. You should never say 'totally.'" I smirked at him, my irritation largely forgotten, what with all the witty banter and his wandering hands.

"I'm a rock star. I can say whatever I want," Chase said.

He nipped my earlobe, then my neck, and his hands were on my ass, and then he was pushing me up against a wall and kissing me. I felt eyes on us, watching us, hating the attention I was getting and they weren't. Or weren't...yet.

I'm so mixed up. I don't know what I want.

Chase sensed me tense. "You're not okay. What is it?"

I shook my head. "Not here, not now. Let's go somewhere."

"There's an after-party uptown. We can talk in the cab on the way."

When we were in the cab and on the way to the after-party, Chase turned to me, his hand resting on my knee. "So talk. What's bugging you?"

How much to tell him? Argh.

"Well, it's just...I was in the bathroom, and I heard these girls talking about you, the same ones who were trying to get you to go their place with them. They were talking about hot you are, which you totally are," I smirked at him as I used his word, "and the one girl was talking about how much she wanted you. Again, understandable. You're basically sex on legs. And the other girl was saying how she knows a girl who hooked up with you after a show, and that you're into some different kind of stuff. And I…I just don't know why it bothered me so much. But that's not true; I do know. It just reminded me that I don't know why I'm here, or what we are, and that I don't have any reason to be jealous. And no, I don't want to try and figure all that shit out right now, I just want to go to the party with you and have fun and celebrate your awesome show."

"Um, wow, okay," Chase said, sitting back with a sigh. "That's a lot of things. I don't even know where to start."

I shrugged and squeezed closer to him. "So don't start. You asked and I told you. I'm really, really not trying to be all girly and talk about my feelings. Mainly because I'm still trying to figure out what I'm feeling. Let's just have a good time."

"But now you have me thinking. Yeah, I hooked up a few times before you got here, but—"

"Chase, for real. Let's not worry about it now."

"But—"

"Chase. Listen to me. Stop thinking like a guy for a second. You don't have to jump in and fix anything. I'm here, you're here…just let it go for now. I'm not ready to talk serious yet."

Chase searched my eyes, then shrugged. "Okay, I guess I get that. Later, though, okay?"

"Sure. Later." *Later, when I've figured out what*

the hell I'm even feeling, much less what I want to do about it.

The after-party was massive. Hundreds of people, band members, fans, techies and roadies and groupies and I didn't even know who else. The huge loft apartment smelled like booze and body heat and cologne and perfume. There was a makeshift bar along one wall and corner, staffed by a catering company, two men and two women, clean-cut, nondescript, and efficient. Alcohol was flowing freely, the noise level nearly deafening. I saw no one I recognized except Chase's band mates: Dave, Austin, and Gage, each of whom I'd met a total of once, when I'd first arrived.

Chase got a vocal welcome, and I felt him turn on the charisma. On the way up, he was just Chase, laid back, quiet, holding my hand. He was still in his battered leather pants, but he'd put on a white linen shirt, the sleeves cut off and the edges artistically frayed, unbuttoned to his navel. Then, as soon as the door opened and we walked into the loft, he transformed into a different person entirely. It was like his entire being just...turned on, and he exuded this powerful, irresistible charm and charisma. He was dynamic, just standing, walking, talking, when in this mode. Every eye was on him, watching him, hoping he'd talk to them. He was funny, entertaining, attentive to the person he was speaking to...

Which meant everyone was looking at me. Judging me. Assessing me. I wanted to let go of Chase's hand, just get away and catch the first flight back to Detroit, away from the attention and the rock star drama. It was ridiculous. I mean, he wasn't even famous yet, and he was being swarmed by people who wanted his attention, and that meant I was being grilled, questioned, chatted up, and flirted with. The women all wanted Chase to notice them, to talk to them, to flirt with them. To take them home. Except, he was with me. He flew me here from Detroit, and brought me to the show and now this party, when he could probably have had any two or three women here, at once.

I didn't know whether to be jealous and upset that he probably had taken multiple women home, or flattered that he liked me enough to want me there, instead of these women. I chose flattered, because it was easier. The jealousy got pushed down and ignored, to be dealt with later.

The party lasted well into the night, or, more accurately, the wee hours of the morning. When things started to blur, I asked Chase to take me home. He seemed like he wasn't ready to leave the party yet, but he did. He made his rounds of good-byes, which took nearly another hour, by which point I was yawning and starting to come down from my buzz.

By the time we got back to Chase's place, I was too tired to do anything but fall asleep. Chase, bless his sweet heart, curled up behind me and let me sleep. My last thought, before succumbing to sleep, was that I'd have to reward him later.

We slept the day through, had a late breakfast/early lunch at a diner a few blocks from Chase's walkup. We talked, a lot. He had a degree in musical theater, oddly enough. He'd almost joined the Army out of high school but hadn't at the last second. I told him about my first boyfriend, the one who'd cheated on me with my best friend's brother. That really messed with my self-esteem, needless to say. He'd told me he'd never really been attracted to me, and had thought it was just because I was fat—his words, not mine. It turned out he wasn't attracted to me because I was fat, and because he was gay. I got over it, mostly. I chalked that one up to bad luck and learned to feel better about myself, to accept my body as uniquely mine, and uniquely beautiful.

Chase spent a long time after that story reminding me how perfect he thought I was. He took me home, brought me to his room, and stripped me slowly, peeling my dress off, kissing my flesh as he bared it.

I stood stock still and let him kiss me, let the touch of his lips on my flesh ignite the always-banked fires of desire within me. He unzipped the back of the dress, brushed the sleeves off my shoulders, and let the dress fall around my feet. Then, standing in front of me, he began at my shoulders, kissing his way down my body. He was slow for once, lingering at my breasts, then down to my belly and my thighs.

By the time he had kissed his way back up to my lips, I was trembling with desire, my nipples hard with need. I wanted him to touch me, wanted to feel him hard against me, feel his hands on me, feel him fill me. His kisses had inflamed my passions, and I had to bite my tongue to keep from begging him.

He hadn't even taken his shirt off, and I found myself aching to touch him. I tugged at the hem of his shirt, but he pushed my hands away.

"Not yet," he said. "Soon."

He went to his dresser and removed a long, wide strip of black cotton. "Trust me?" When I nodded, he wrapped the blindfold around my eyes and tied it in back. "Can you see?"

I couldn't. I fought back an initial rush of panic. It was loosely tied, and my hands were free so I could pull it off if I wanted to. I forced myself to relax and focus on the other senses.

I had the aftertaste of dinner in my mouth: corned beef Reuben and fries with a Coke. I heard a rasping metallic click and then the tiny whump of the flame coming to life from a lighter, then the snap and pop of a wick catching: a candle being lit; these sounds were repeated several more times. I smelled the candles, smelled Chase—male sweat, faint cologne, leather. I was aware of Chase moving around the room, hearing his footsteps on the old, creaking hardwood floors, following his smell and the intangible feeling of his presence. Now he moved close to me, not touching me.

Goosebumps pebbled my flesh, on my arm, and then my side, a strange, not-quite physical sensation. It moved from my side and down my hip and my leg, and then back up the other leg.

"What is that?" I asked. "What are you doing to me?"

"Guess."

"I can't figure it out. It's like—god, it's weird!" Then it hit me. "You're not touching me, but almost, right? Moving your hand right next to my skin but not actually making contact."

"Bingo."

He rewarded me with a leisurely removal of my bra. No other part of him touched me except his hands on my back as he unclasped the hooks. Not being touched had never been so erotic. I tried to anticipate where he'd put his hands next, but he always managed to surprise me. He slid the straps of my bra off my shoulder, and I expected to feel his hands on my breasts, perhaps skimming underneath to heft their weight, or rolling a nipple; he kissed my back where the strap had been, a slow tonguing kiss across my back. I felt his hair tickle the back of my left arm as he moved across my body. I lifted my arm as he kept circling around, planting kisses as he went, and then he was kissing the side of my breast, one hand on the small of my back, the other wrapped around one leg, kissing, kissing; he was kneeling next to me, I realized. He still hadn't touched my nipple, or removed my panties. I was tingling everywhere, every inch of my flesh burning with anticipation of his touch, his kiss. My folds were wet, waiting, wanting.

I put my hands in his soft hair, smelling of shampoo and pomade. His hand on my leg finally, finally slipped up to dip beneath the leg hem of my panties, pushing up to the crease of my hip, achingly near my wet, hot core, where I wanted his touch so badly. I was trembling, waiting for him to move just an inch to the right.

He pulled his hand free, and I moaned in dismay. He tugged the waistband of my panties down enough to kiss a fiery line across my hip bone to my belly just above my sex, slow, hot kisses that had my knees buckling.

Just a little lower, please!

"Soon, baby," he said.

I'd spoken aloud without realizing it. "Please, Chase. Touch me. Kiss me."

He just chuckled as he kissed my opposite hip, then down my leg, pulling my panties down as he went, a single centimeter at a time, it seemed, agonizingly slow. Then, after an eternity of torturous delight, my panties were off and tossed aside, and he was kissing up my calf, holding the leg in both hands, sliding his palms up my thighs to cup my ass, kneading the muscle. I spread my legs apart as he neared my groin, lips now mid-thigh and still rising, and yes, oh, please...

I nearly fell backward when he lapped at my pussy with a long swipe of his tongue across the labia. I moaned, tangled my fingers in his hair, and let my head fall backward. He held my ass in both hands as he kissed and licked, flicked and tongued, moved his head from side to side and up and down. I felt my legs dipping in the rhythm of his mouth's motion, helpless to stop myself, and now the fires were raging out of control, burning and exploding, my muscles tensing in preparation for the imminent explosion....

He moved away, and I whimpered. "I was so close—why'd you stop?" I sounded whiny in that moment, but I didn't care, I wanted his mouth on me again, or his hands.

I reached out and felt the empty air around me, but he'd moved out of reach. I smelled for him, listened for him, simply felt for his presence, but he was nowhere my senses could find.

I heard his voice, over to my right, against what would be the closet wall. "Take two steps back."

I hesitated. "Where am I going?" I thought about the layout of the room, and answered my own question. "The bed, right?"

"Two steps, and then stop."

I took one step backward, then another, and felt the edge of the bed bump the back of my knees. I stopped, and waited. My heart thudded in my chest, and I smelled his hair before I felt his presence. My four other senses had never been so sharp as now without my sight. I felt his fingers brush my belly, barely contact at all, a whispering touch, like feathers, or a breath; I gasped and shivered.

The feather-light touch turned to a gentle but unmistakable push. I leaned back to sit on the bed. Chase kissed my kneecap, and my thigh, and then I was falling backward, lying down with my legs hanging off the bed. A hand clasped around my wrist and extended it above my head. Then, beginning at my palm, Chase kissed his way down my arm. I sucked in my breath when he reached my breast, slipping his lips around its circumference, narrowing to my aching, stiffened nipple. He only lingered there for a moment, grazing it with his teeth but once. I wanted to crush his head to my breast, or guide his hand to my pussy, or simply beg him to touch me, touch me. I didn't, though. The game, the drawn-out, rapturous, torture was exquisite.

He repeated the process for my other arm, lifting it above my head and kissing his way down to my breast. This time, however, instead of merely moving away from my breast, he kept lapping and licking downward, tracing the lines of my ribs, the hollow of my diaphragm, the expanse of my belly. All the while his hands were brushing and whisking and whispering across my skin, just the pads of his fingertips touching now, and then his palm circling the taut peak of my nipple.

His tongue found my drenched, throbbing folds again, dipped in to pull from my trembling lips a moan of relief. Yes, now he would let me release, now...

He tongued my clit until I was writhing on the bed, sight gone, the only sound my voice, the only scent the musk of my arousal, lost in tactile ecstasy, so close, so close, wavering on the verge, teetering on the brink...one last touch of his tongue...

I grabbed wildly for him when he pulled away again, and he only laughed. My entire body was on fire, quivering with need, primed and set for explosion. My senses were so attuned now that I could hear the rustle of his pants legs as he moved, hear the soft susurrus of his breathing. Every inch of my flesh was on fire, waiting for the next place he would kiss or touch me.

I heard the leather of his pants zipping as he moved to stand next to me. "Sit up and turn to face my voice."

I did as he'd instructed, wondering what was next; he took my hands in his and placed them on his chest. I could feel his heart pounding under my palm. He moved my fingers so I felt a button on his shirt. I realized what he wanted and complied eagerly, unbuttoning his shirt and pushing it off. I wanted to rip his pants off, but, according to the way he was playing this game, I made myself wait. Instead, I explored his torso with my hands, all my attention now focused on my fingers. I traced each muscle, each line and angle and curve from shoulder to wrist to abdomen, lingering, and now I couldn't stop myself from replacing fingers with lips. I kissed him slowly, deliberately. Each time I neared the V-cut above the waistband of his pants, I lingered, let my fingers toy with the button.

When he was shaking and tense, I slipped the button free and unzipped his pants. I moved with delicate attention, following the muscles downward, pushing the pants away inch by inch. I stripped them off then, unable to wait any longer. He was in his boxers now, and I let my hands learn the shape of his body through the underwear, the curved stone of his buttocks, the hard angles of his hips, the rigid shaft of his straining cock. He'd leaked a dot of moisture at his tip. I moved his box-er-briefs down on one hip, licked the hollow where leg met hip bone, then across until my lips were brushing next to his cock. He sucked his stomach in, a reflexive motion of anticipation. Instead of touching him yet, I revealed his other hip, mirrored the kiss across his groin.

Now, at last, I tugged the elastic over his cock, slipping him into my mouth as I exposed him. He gasped as I took him into my throat, groaned when I wrapped my fingers around him, and rumbled deep in his chest when I bobbed my head and moved my hands along his shaft. I sucked until my cheeks hollowed, sliding my hands on him faster and faster, his hips bucking him into my mouth.

His breathing was ragged, and he was buckling at the knees.

"Oh, god, I'm gonna come," he said.

I let go immediately and moved back on the bed, lying down on my back and waiting, legs spread in invitation. I heard him growling, imagined him flexing every muscle in an effort to hold back.

"You didn't come, did you?" I asked. "You better not have. I want you to come inside me."

He groaned again, and I felt weight on the bed. "No, but nearly."

"Good. I want you inside me, right now. Please, Chase."

I reached for him, where I thought he was. I felt hair, took a handful, and pulled gently until I could reach his jaw, and then his shoulder and then his hip, and then he was above me. I grasped his cock in my fist and guided him to my entrance.

"No more games. Just take me," I rocked my hips as I spoke, and he sank into me.

He shuddered, tensed, and I felt his lips brush mine, shaking as he held himself back from the edge.

"God, you feel so good," he whispered, "I'm there already again, I can't…" He sounded ragged, desperate.

The feeling of him inside me, filling me past full, knowing he was so close, it brought me in a single rush, before he'd thrust even once, to the edge of climax. I tangled my fingers in his hair and pulled his head down to mine, crushed my lips to his. I thrust my tongue into his mouth and as I did so, rolled my hips against him, driving him to the hilt.

He held himself stone-still, every muscle tensed. He was still holding back.

"Give it to me," I breathed, rocking into him, one hand still gripping his hair, the other clawing down his back. "Don't hold back anymore. Give it to me. Hard. Now."

He roared, a feral sound, leonine, primal, and bucked his hips, sliding his cock into me, once, deep, and hard. Again. Again. I gasped, bit his shoulder. He arched his back outward, pulling almost out and tensing, holding. Still withholding. I dug my nails into his hips and jerked him toward me, pulling with all my strength against his resistance. Still he played the game, holding back.

I rolled sideways and he went with me, pulling me over him. I draped myself on top of him, waiting, let him fade back from the edge. The game continued. Above him like this, I held the power of pace. He was sunk to the hilt, our hip bones grinding. I sat straight, stretching him backward, placed my hands on his belly, my weight spread between his body and my knees. I waited, absorbing the sensations rocketing through me: his cock, hard and huge and throbbing with pent-up pressure, his body beneath me, muscles tense and rock-solid, his hands resting on my hips, my heart beating wildly in my chest like a fleeing rabbit, my nerve endings all afire now, silence except our breathing, the scent of sex thick in the air.

I lifted up, just a few inches, held my weight there for a moment, and then sank down. I gasped, he groaned. More. I lifted higher, sank back down harder, hips thumping, blood thrumming. He growled again. I felt his buttocks clench against my thighs.

"Give it to me," I said, leaning close to his face. "I want it."

"No," he said, crashing his lips to mine and spearing his tongue into my mouth. "Make me."

I rocked up and back down. "With…pleasure…"

No rhythm, only sporadic rolls of my hips, a pause, lift up and sink down. His hands found my breasts, pinched my nipples, sending jags of lightning bursting through me. Then he cheated. He dug a single finger between our merged bodies and found my clit somehow. I rocked back instinctively, lifted up, gave him access.

A few slow circles drove me mad; he moved his finger faster, and then I came, almost without warning, a nuclear detonation blasting through every cell of my body.

I couldn't stop the rhythm then. I fell onto him, clutched him against me, and let my hips run wild.

Hips don't lie, as the song goes, and mine danced on his with truthful desperation. I couldn't play the game any longer. I whimpered against his neck as I pulsed my pussy onto him.

He arched his back upward, arms wrapped around me, clinging to me as he came. I was still riding my first climax, and when he came I soared over the edge again, the heat of his release washing through me, each piston-drive of his cock sending me further and further into a frenzy of orgasm. We were bucking in syncopated abandon now, riding each other beyond climax, beyond mere physical release into something else, into an escape from singular self into a duality of ecstasy.

We were caught up in a storm, and all we could do was cling to each other through it, let it pound through us. When it passed, we were both limp and panting, sweating, spent.

I rolled off him and nestled into his arms, feeling his heart beat against my cheek.

We showered, changed, and Chase hailed a cab but wouldn't tell me where we were going. The cab pulled up to Macy's.

"What are we doing here?" I asked.

"Shopping," was his cryptic reply.

"Well, no shit, it's the world's largest department store. Shopping for what?"

He just grinned. It seemed a bit like a leer, honestly, lecherous and eager for what he had planned. I rolled my eyes at him and let him drag me by the hand up the escalators and to the lingerie department.

"Lingerie? Really?" I stopped at the entrance to the lingerie department.

"Yes, really."

"Are you saying my underwear aren't sexy enough for you?" I teased.

"I'm saying you can never have too much sexy lingerie."

We browsed together, Chase showing me what he liked, always grabbing an item several sizes too small. Eventually, we settled on a red and black lace bustier with matching panties, and a hot pink and purple ruffled set.

I tried a few of the less adventurous bras, and then stepped back out, fully dressed, with an idea.

It was near closing time and the store was empty, with one store assistant prowling around. I waited until she was sorting through a stack of panties on the other side of the department, then pulled Chase with me into the changing room.

I stripped for him, peeling off my clothes to a silent rhythm, then pinned him against the stall wall with my body. I was down to just my panties, rubbing my bare breasts against the soft cotton of his shirt. I felt his cock burgeon in his pants, met his gaze as I unzipped him.

"Hello? Is anyone still in here?" the store clerk called out.

"Yes," I said. Chase had frozen, not even breathing. "I'm just trying on a few last things. I'll be done in a minute."

"We're closing in five minutes. If you're going to make a purchase, it needs to be soon."

"Okay, I'll be right out." I stifled a laugh, tugging Chase's underwear down to free his erection.

I glided my hand on his length, put my mouth to his ear and whispered, "I want you right now." I felt Chase's cock throb and tense as I spoke. "Put it in my pussy."

I stroked him, one hand massaging his sack, until he was rolling his hips into my hand. When he was nearly ready, I stripped my panties off one leg and faced the wall, bending at the waist with my hands braced.

Chase didn't need another invitation. He slipped a finger into me, finding me already wet. He plunged into me, and we both had to bite our lips to stifle our moans.

"Hello? I really need to cash out, dear," came the clerk's voice. Her shoes peeked under the door, tiny little white sneakers, the footwear of a woman who spends her life on her feet.

I was just within reach of the top of the door. Chase had frozen, and I plunged my hips back into him to get him moving. The exhilaration of this moment, being completely naked, with Chase's cock driving into me from behind, and only a thin stall door between us and complete humiliation...I nearly came right then. I caught up the hangers of the items I wanted and hung them over the door.

"Ring these up, and I'll be right out to pay," I said. My voice wasn't quite steady, but she didn't say anything, if she'd noticed.

Chase was moving slowly, trying to avoid making any noises as our bodies joined. I was riding the edge of climax now, and so was Chase.

"Will that be cash or charge?"

God, the woman was relentless. *Leave me alone for five seconds!*

Chase handed me a wad of cash, and I passed it over the top of the door.

"I don't know how much it'll be, but that should cover it," I said, a little breathless.

The clerk took the cash and finally left us alone.

"Now, Chase!" I whispered. "Come for me, right now!"

I drove my ass onto him, feeling him plunge hard to the hilt deep inside my pussy. Again, even harder, and the stall shook. A third time, and I rocked backward to absorb the impact, feeling him drive deeper than he'd ever been, both of us silent, breath caught. I felt him tense, drive one last time into me, and then he was coming, flooding me with his seed. I felt him come and I joined him an instant later, resting my head against the wall as he fluttered into me, my inner muscles clenching around him in spasms.

He pulled out of me, tucked himself back into his pants, and slumped back against the wall. "Damn, Anna...just...damn."

I smirked at him, feeling sated and daring. I dug in my purse for a little packet of tissues, and cleaned myself before dressing again. I told Chase to stay in the dressing room until I called him.

I walked up to the cashier's stand, my thighs quivering with aftershocks. I could barely walk, but I had to cover up and act as if nothing had happened. The woman, mercifully, had everything bagged up and the change ready, and she vanished into a back room with barely a "thank you."

I sneaked Chase out of the changing room, and we left Macy's, laughing like teenagers.

After Macy's we went to Times Square and min-
gled with the bustling crowd, holding hands and
walking aimlessly. We sat on the giant steps with
the signs around us, kissing as if we were alone,
making out until even the New Yorkers shouted at
us to get a room.

We spent the entire following day in the recording studio. I sat in the producer's booth, watching in rapt interest as they laid down track after
track, sometimes going back for a dozen takes of
the same section of song, the same riff, the same
vocalization until they got it right.

I knew my way around a mixing/EQ board, and
I quickly learned to understand what the producers
and sound engineers were doing at the giant board
on the other side of the acoustic room.

The whole process made me wonder if I could
ever find my way on the other side of the glass,
where Chase and his band was. I'd always loved
singing, and had settled on DJing as a way of
utilizing my musical talent, modest as it seemed
to me. As any girl with a decent voice does, I'd
harbored dreams of "being a singer," but as I got
older and learned a bit about the business, I came
to realize how distant and unlikely a prospect
that was. Now, sitting in a real recording studio,
in New York City, no less, those dreams all came
rushing back to me.

I was lost in my thoughts and was startled when Chase came up behind me and kissed me on the neck.

"Thinking deep thoughts, huh?" he asked.

"What? Oh, yeah. Guess so. I didn't hear you come in."

"I called your name twice, babe. You were zoned out. What were you thinking about?"

I looked up at him over my shoulder. "Oh, just how cool it is to be here, in a studio. Thanks for bringing me."

"Thought you might like it." He glanced at the producer, a younger-looking man with full-sleeve tattoos on both arms and wide-gauge earrings. "We have a few minutes left on our time, right, Jake?"

Jake nodded, glancing at his watch. "Yeah, a couple. Wanna lay down a bonus track with your girl?"

Chase just gestured to the door to the booth. "Shall we?"

We sat down in the booth, and Chase settled the expensive headphones on my ears.

"What do you want to sing?" Chase asked.

I thought carefully. I didn't know if they were going to actually include this recording on the CD or not, but if they did, I wanted it to be knock-out.

"I don't suppose you know 'Don't You Wanna Stay,' do you?" I asked Chase.

"Jason Aldean and Kelly Clarkston? Surprisingly enough, I do," Chase answered, with a sheepish grin. "I learned it when I did a karaoke contest with a friend. We actually won with that song."

The producer tapped at the computer keyboard for a moment, and then the introductory strains filled my ears through the headphones. Chase started it off, the slow, sad melody turned aching and haunting by his clear, powerful voice. *He really is amazing*, I reflected. I heard my part coming up, and Chase nodded to me. I took a deep breath and added my voice to his, and once again I felt that intangible, bone-deep knowledge boil in my blood. We were on, we were hitting it just right, our natural chemistry and talent flowing together. I could see the producer nodding, a surprised expression on his face. We were killing it.

I felt my skin prickle and adrenaline surge through me, felt the notes flow from me without thought, without effort. Chase's hand was in mine, and then my eyes closed and all I knew was the music and those wonderful lyrics, which had suddenly taken on new meaning.

Every kiss we'd shared filled the spaces of my mind, every moment spent naked together, every look—it all took on new importance. I really had no clue what this was with Chase, or how long it would last.

The song ended all too soon, and Chase and I ripped the headphones off to embrace each other.

"That rocked!" Jake said. "Chase, your girl's got some real pipes on her. I may have to steal her one of these days. For music, I mean."

"You just want to steal her, period," Chase said, with a wry grin.

Jake shrugged. "Yeah, well, you'd better get out of here before I do. Good work, guys."

We left the studio to have a late dinner, and I had the song running through my head the entire time, as well as the thoughts the lyrics had engendered. Chase must have sensed my pensive mood.

"What's up, buttercup? You seem lost in thought again." He pushed back from his plate and searched my eyes from over the top of his glass of beer.

I shrugged. "Oh, that song has just always had a lot of meaning for me. It always makes me think, I guess."

"So what are you thinking now?"

I still wasn't sure if I wanted to have that conversation with Chase yet, if at all. It was too easy to just float along one day at a time and let the relationship, such as it was, be a nameless, uncategorized thing. To put a box around it, to give it a name and boundaries, would be to change it.

After a long, thoughtful silence, I shook my head. "Nothing. Nothing important."

Chase frowned. "You know we have to talk eventually, Anna."

"No, we don't. One day at a time. *Carpe diem* and all that."

He laughed, a mirthless, resigned sound. "Isn't this backward? Aren't I supposed to be the one avoiding the discussion?"

I shrugged again, a coward's non-answer. "How about another beer and then we go back to your place?"

Back in his bedroom, we lay down, fully clothed, on his bed, just holding each other. The avoided conversation loomed between us. It really was backward, him being the one who wanted to put a name to what we were, to establish our thing together as a relationship. I didn't want to do that. Why I didn't want to was a more complicated thing, and that's what I ruminated on as I lay in Chase's arms, content to be held for the moment.

Why didn't I want to commit to this being an actual relationship, monogamous and working toward some kind of future together? Chase was incredible. He was charming and thoughtful, gorgeous, talented...an amazing lover. He was going places, career-wise. He wanted me. That was a big one. He wanted me. I'd still not quite gotten over that. I think I was expecting it to change at some point, for him to wake up and realize he did in fact want a girl who was not me, who was in some way either more or less than me, depending on how you looked at it. But he hadn't so far, and judging by his response to my avoiding the relationship discussion, he wanted more with me. Something long-term.

Why wasn't I jumping at that?

Jeff.

I'd left something unfinished with him, back in Detroit. I hadn't said when, or if, I was coming back. I'd just left, perhaps precipitately. I'd hurt him. That was clear in his eyes, in the tense slump of his shoulders when he drove me home.

He'd never said what he wanted with me. But he hadn't needed to. It was clear, somehow. Jeff had a way of implying his desires without saying them, of communicating his thoughts nonverbally. I couldn't have pinpointed what it was he'd done, or how he'd looked at me that told me he wanted a relationship, but I knew he did. Maybe it was the fact that he'd had a crush on me for all the years we worked together, never voicing it, never moving on it after a few initial, hesitant flirty moments I'd pretended not to notice. Maybe it was his slow, sweet, reverent lovemaking.

I shut down thoughts of that. I couldn't let my mind go there, not when I was in Chase's bed.

The realization hit me like a ton of bricks: I had to choose. Stay there, indefinitely, and eventually decide that I was staying with Chase. Or I had to go back to Detroit and face Jeff. That's what had been niggling at me since I'd arrived in New York. I didn't know how to choose. I didn't know what I wanted. Who I wanted, long-term, if either of them.

"Quit thinking so hard and just be here with me," Chase said.

"Are you a mind-reader?"

He turned into me and kissed my cheek, then my chin. "Sometimes. You wear your thoughts on your face, though, so that makes it easier. You're thinking too hard. We don't have to figure anything out. Just be here with me, in this moment, right now."

I nodded, his stubble scratching my temple. "You're right. I'm sorry, I'm just—"

"Let it go for now."

I lifted up on an elbow. "So distract me."

Our lips met, a hesitant touch at first, almost as tender as if it were our first kiss. Slow, and delicate. Explorative. It wasn't a kiss meant to go anywhere, at first. It was just meant to be a kiss, the expression of affection. His kiss told me what he felt about me. His lips showed me in a visceral way that he thought I was valuable, and beautiful.

The feeling of being desired, the knowledge that a man as hot as Chase thought I was beautiful… that was something I couldn't ever get enough of. I still couldn't turn off my brain, even kissing Chase like this. He had unlocked something inside me that night in his bedroom in Detroit. He'd unleashed something powerful and insatiable. He'd made me understand my own worth as a sexual woman. There was a phrase I'd heard a million times before but never really truly grasped until this moment in Chase's New York apartment:

He'd shown me my inner goddess.

I did feel, in that moment, with his arms slipping around me, his body sliding against mine, his fingers exploring my body and starting the slow unwrapping of my clothes, that I was a goddess. I had power. My body, my desires, my needs...I could affect a man, hold sway over him, manipulate him or lift him up or draw his pleasure out, multiply it, deepen it. I could, for the minutes or hours I was with a man in bed, be all of his universe, the only thing that mattered in his existence, in those moments. It's not about experience or lack thereof, or what you've learned or with whom. That power comes from within a woman, and it must be understood on a blood- and bone- and soul-deep level.

Time had vanished and reappeared, and I was naked with him, limbs tangling in a writhing twist of flesh and sweat and heat. I had no memory of removing clothes, of anything but his lips and his hands and his body against mine, and it didn't matter. Nothing mattered. Only him, only me, only us together.

There were no games, no kinks, no blindfolds or positions or bindings, just bodies mingling and merging. Lips collided and tongues mated, hands and legs and arms wrapped and touched and twined. I felt him move into me, fill me, glide with serpentine grace to merge our bodies in a manner more intimate than ever before. Walls and defenses and worries melted away, futures and pasts and choices had no meaning.

Climax happened gradually, together. We mounted the heights of pleasure together in a time-less dance of flesh, moving and breathing until we were left motionless and breathless together.

There was something massively important in that experience together. I couldn't look at it too carefully, not yet. I just let it permeate my being, sweep my thoughts away. His breathing and mine matched, slowed, deepened, merged until there was nothing but breath, nothing but contact of cooling flesh and drowsing mind.

We slept then, and dreamed no dreams but of each other.

I stood in the shadow of a curtain backstage, watching Chase and his band Six Foot Tall per-form. We were in a tiny club outside Hoboken, New Jersey, and the crowd was wild, raucous, and rambunctious. They demanded hard numbers, fast beats, and constant spectacle. Chase seemed to instinctively know he couldn't try to bring the tempo down, but kept the band playing their hardest original numbers as well as some stock cover songs.

I could tell they were exhausted from the intense pace of the show. Chase was dripping sweat, wiping his face with a rag between numbers and guzzling bottles of water. He spent a lot of the show at the edge of the stage, hanging off the speakers and getting as close to the crowd as possible.

By the time two hours had passed, they were out of original material and had played all the stock hard rock covers they knew. The stage lights had been doused and the band had thanked the crowd for coming out, but the little club was being rocked by chants of "encore, encore, encore!" As minutes passed and the band failed to reappear, the crowd became increasingly restless.

Finally, Chase turned to me. "I don't know what to do. We're out of material except ballads and soft shit they won't want to hear."

"Well, at this point, if that's all you have left, that's what you have to do, right?" I peeked out at the crowd. "They sound like they're about to riot. You guys have to play something."

Chase stared at me, then snapped his fingers and pointed at me. "I've got it. Come on."

He pulled me by the hand onto the stage, the lights still down. The band took their places, waiting for Chase to announce what they would play.

He turned to me. "You still know how to sing 'Broken'?"

I nodded, numb. "Yeah, of course, but—"

He pointed at the guitarist. "Start it up, bro."

The guitarist nodded, his long braided beard wagging. His fingers slid down the fretboard, and he picked out the opening notes. The bassist rolled his shoulders, and then joined in, thumping the rhythm. The drummer waited another beat, then *ratatatted* in on the snare.

A techie garbed in black scurried out onstage and handed me a cordless mic, and then the stage lights came on, bathing Chase and me in a single spotlight. I looked out at the crowd, the faces swathed in shadows, heads bobbing to the familiar song. Scattered cheers and applause met us as the band ramped up into high gear, and then music was washing through me and my rush of nerves receded.

I had a sudden flash of the first time I'd done this song with Chase, in an appropriately named bar called The Dive. Then, we'd sung to a karaoke track in front of maybe a hundred people. Now, the club was stuffed to the rafters, easily three hundred people packed in tight, holding clear plastic cups of pale amber beer over their heads, sloshing it over the rims as they jumped and cheered.

Chase started the first verse, and then my voice lifted and wove around his, finding the harmony as if we'd practiced a dozen times. The natural onstage chemistry Chase and I shared kicked in, sparks buzzing between us, and then everything faded away but the driving guitars and the chugging base and the pounding drums and Chase's blazing brown eyes locked on mine.

We bridged from the chorus to the second verse, and the crowd was wilder than ever. Chase took my hand as we finished the song, and I felt a brief, sharp pang of sharp emotion burn through me, mixed-up feelings of awe for Chase's natural ability to play the crowd, adrenaline at the experience of performing on an actual stage with his band, and something awfully like deep affection for Chase.

The song ended, the lights went down, and the crowd continued to cheer. Chase pulled me off the stage, as elated with post-performance adrenaline as I was. The band was behind us, chattering and clapping each other on the back.

Chase ignored the band and the still cheering crowd, pulling me toward the red and white exit sign. He pushed open the door and led me out into the warm summer night. The alley behind the bar was dark and silent, lit only by the ambient city lights and the half moon.

The alley was filled by the cargo van the band used to transport their equipment, and Chase led me to a patch of darker shadows between the wall of the club and the white metal of the van. He pushed me back up against the wall and crushed his lips to mine, heat billowing off him, sweat from his upper lip mingling with my own, his mouth cold from the water he'd slammed on the way out to the alley. His body pressed against me, pinning me to the wall, and his hands moved from cupping my face as he kissed me, smoothing down my body to the heavy curve of my breasts, and farther, to the hem of my skirt just above my knees.

His cock was a hard rod between us, and the furious fire of his kiss lit the boiling fuel of my desire, turned into a white-hot blaze by the rush of adrenaline. I reached between us and opened his leather pants, pushed them down, curled greedy fingers around the silky steel of his shaft. He dragged my thong down and I stepped out of the panties as they dropped to the ground between us.

His fingers delved into my pussy, already wet and aching for him, not needing any priming. I lifted my leg and wrapped it around his waist, and he held it in place with one hand. I gripped his cock in my hand and guided him to my quivering entrance, bit his lower lip as he penetrated into me. He lifted up on his toes to drive himself inside me to the hilt, holding me aloft with one hand around my leg and the other around my ass, pulling me tight against him.

Our lips met, crushed together but not kissing, breath merging as Chase drove up into me, rocking his body upward, spearing me until my breath caught. I buried my face in his neck, nipped his skin, muffled a gasp against the salt of his flesh, holding on to his shoulders and whimpering.

Within a dozen thrusts I was reaching climax, the leg supporting me buckling under the pressure of the ecstasy driving through me.

"Oh, god, Chase, I'm coming," I gasped, clinging to him, breathing the words in his ear.

Hearing me say that spurred Chase to move even harder, lifting up on his toes, pushing me back into the wall with every thrust of his cock inside me. I came on an up-thrust, biting his shoulder to muffle a shriek, biting hard enough to draw a grunt of pain from Chase, which turned into a drawn-out groan as he came. He plowed into me, harder and harder, his mouth huffing loud moaning breaths into my hair as he shot his seed into me, a flood of heat washing against my walls.

My inner muscles locked around his cock as I came, my body trembling and quivering and shaking, every nerve on fire, my arms and legs shaking from a mixture of pleasure and exhaustion.

Chase finished, slowed his thrusting, and pulled out of me, letting my leg down. We both leaned back against the cold metal of the van just as Chase's band-mates came out into the alley looking for us. I tugged my skirt down mere seconds before they shoved the door open, but our out-of-breath panting and just-fucked hair gave away what we'd been doing. They just grinned and shook their heads as they lit cigarettes, which drove Chase and me—both non-smokers—back inside to look for drinks.

I visited the bathroom to clean up and then met Chase at the bar, where he had a Jameson and ginger ale waiting for me. I sat next to him, realizing I'd left my panties on the ground in the alley. We drank with the rest of the band until the bar closed, fans surrounding us, everyone wanting to party with the band. The other guys continued on to an after-party, but this time Chase took me back to his place.

We rode each other again, this time more slowly, our moans of united climax rising in harmony.

It was nearly dawn before we finally fell asleep.

For the first time since arriving in New York, I found myself alone for several hours. Chase's band had to rehearse their set for that night's show, and since I was going to see it later anyway, Chase suggested I "do some shopping or whatever."

I decided to do the tourist thing. I'd been to New York a few times before, but I'd never really just explored; I'd always been with friends or family with a set itinerary. This time, I went to the Statue of Liberty, explored the area around Times Square on foot, ate at a hole-in-the-wall pizzeria, took the subway in a circle around the boroughs, just wasting time and seeing the everyday-life parts of the city.

I made it back to Chase's apartment with enough time to take a nap, shower, and change. Well, that was the idea, at least. I got the nap in, exhausted from a long day on foot, but the shower didn't exactly happen as planned.

Chase came back from rehearsal, amped up and adrenalized. The hot, leisurely shower I'd anticipated turned into Chase pinning me under the stream of water, one of my legs around his hip as he drove up into me. There was no romance or technique to it, this time. Chase often spent an inordinate amount of time giving me pleasure before he let himself go; this time, the focus was on him, and I liked it that way, in that moment. I tangled my arms around his neck and held tight as he drilled into me, grunting, plunging. He was primal, raw power. He came with a shudder and a growl of teeth in my shoulder.

We finished cleaning up and toweled off, and by that time, Chase was ready again. He didn't make any overt moves to take me again, but I could tell he wanted it.

I waited until he had gotten his boxers on before I made my move. He was pulling his shirt over his head and momentarily blind. I knelt in front of him, jerked his boxers around his knees, and wrapped my lips around his head, letting my teeth lightly graze him, enough to shock. He gasped and flinched.

"God...what are you doing?" Chase tugged the shirt and looked down at me as I stroked his base. "We just went...and I have to be at the club in a few minutes..."

I licked him from root to tip before answering. "If you don't have time, then I guess..." I backed away slowly, giving him time to consider.

"Well, we might have a few minutes," he said.

"I thought so. I mean, I wouldn't want you to perform...frustrated." I used both hands then, pumping him slowly, just the very tip in my mouth, sucking gently.

Chase tried to answer, but could only gasp as I slid him deeper into my throat, moving my hands down his length as I did so. His fingers tangled in my damp hair and he fluttered his hips, restraining himself from thrusting. I went slow for a moment, stroking, sucking, and massaging, until he was limp-kneed and gasping. He was slick and hard in my hands, veins throbbing and sac taut, ready to burst. I moved a fist on him, quickly now, a finger massaging the muscles of his taint, lips locked around his engorged head. He threw his head back, groaning, tightened his fingers in my hair, and then he couldn't help his thrusting hips. I took him deep, not quite gagging as he brushed the back of my throat. Harder, faster, until he was dipping at the knees and rocking his hips to the rhythm of my bobbing.

"God, goddamn...I'm coming..."

I hadn't needed the warning. I could feel him tense, feel his balls contract and release in my palm. He came hard, shooting a jet of hot, thick, salty come down my throat, and then again, and a third time. I kept moving, kept sucking, until he was curled down over his belly and rumbling, jerking. He lifted me up to my feet and held me in a hug, breathing hard.

"Wow, what was that for?" Chase asked.

I shrugged. "I wanted to. I like making you feel good, especially before your show. If you guys kill it like you did the other day, I might even do it again."

Chase chuckled. "Well, then, we'll have to kill it, won't we?"

They opened for one of New York's biggest up-and-coming local bands, and they killed it. They started their set with one of their hardest numbers, a thrash piece that had the crowd moshing within minutes. That set the pace for the rest of the show, each song harder than the last, and the crowd ate it up. Chase was in rare form, climbing up on a stack of speakers for an entire number, getting the

crowd participating in chant-back choruses, jumping off the stage and working through the crowd,
even singing from on top of the bar at one point.

By the time their set was over, the crowd was
in a frenzy, and actually demanding an encore.
After approving it with the stage manager, Chase
and the band went back out and did a cover of the
Ramones' "Blitzkrieg Bop."

I had watched from the bar, wanting to experience the show from a different angle. When they finished their set, I made my to the backstage entrance.
Chase had introduced me to the stage staff before
the show. I saw the other guys from the band near
the door to the alley, and I made my way to them.

"Hey, Anna!" Gage, the bassist, greeted me
with an effusive hug.

"Great show, guys!" I said.

I congratulated all of them, then looked around
for Chase, but didn't see him.

"Where's Chase?" I asked.

Gage shifted from one foot to the other, not
meeting my eyes, glancing at the back door to the
alley and then away. "He's...in the bathroom."

My stomach dropped. I suddenly knew what
I'd find if I opened the alley door, but I didn't want
to believe it.

I'd spent the show amazed at Chase's talent,
wondering again what my holdup was with him.

I'd come backstage with the intent of telling him I was planning to stay in New York for a while longer, maybe even having the relationship discussion tomorrow.

"The bathroom?" I narrowed my eyes at Gage, fist clenched. "Don't bullshit me, Gage. Where is he?"

Gage shifted again, biting at his lip ring. "Just give him a minute, Anna."

I shoved Gage out of the way and wrenched the door open. The metal knob was cold in my fist, squeaking as I turned it. The door was heavy, solid and rusted. I put my shoulder to it and pushed. It burst free, sending me stumbling into the alley.

I heard Chase's voice. "Wait, girls, not here, not now, just wait...I don't want Anna to find me—"

My heart clenched and my eyes burned. Chase was backed up against the alley wall, the same two girls from the bathroom at the last show pawing at him. One of them was kneeling in front of him, stopped in the act of opening his pants. The other had his hand in hers against her breast, which was bared, her camisole pulled down.

"Too late," I said, barely above a whisper.

"Anna, wait, please! It's not like you think!" Chase pushed the girls away and stumbled toward me.

I shook my head, spun on my heel, and stomped out of the alley toward the main street. My eyes burned and blurred, and my chest seemed to be clutched in a vise. I heard Chase behind me, calling my name, begging me to wait, trying to explain.

I saw a cab trundle past, lit up. I ran toward it, whistling with two fingers. The cab stopped and let me in. I managed get "airport" out before shattering into sobs. I heard a palm slap the window, saw Chase through tear-blurred eyes, running after the cab, panic on his face.

"Want me to stop for him, lady?" the cabbie asked.

"No. Keep going."

"None of my business, but he looks awful shook up. Sure you don't wanna give him a chance?" I saw the cabbie's pale brown eyes meet mine in the rearview mirror.

"Just fucking drive, goddamn it."

The cabbie shrugged and kept silent the rest of the way to the airport. I didn't have my suitcase, but there was nothing vital in it anyway. He could keep it. I had my purse, my phone, my charger, and my ticket. My phone buzzed and rang nonstop, text after text, voicemail after voicemail. Eventually I turned it off and tried not to have a panic attack.

By some miracle, I made the next flight home.

I cried all the way back to Detroit, soft, silent tears dripping down my chin.

Big Girls Do It on Top

I'M NOT THE CRYING TYPE. I've been through too much in my life to go bawling every time something shitty happens. I cried when my dad died a few years ago, and I cried when my dog died when I was thirteen. Not much else in between, mainly because everything else in my life just kept coming, one thing after another, and if I started crying, I'd never have stopped.

I sobbed all the way from New York to Detroit. I did it quietly, face to the window. My seat mate, an older woman with salt and pepper hair and a ridiculously adorable button nose, asked me what was wrong, but I just shrugged and kept my face to the window, watching the clouds pass by. She sighed and muttered something rude, then went back to her issue of *People*.

I wasn't sure exactly what I was going to do in Detroit. I knew I had to face Jeff, but I couldn't bear the thought of doing so right away. I knew I'd hurt him badly. I knew he'd be pissed when I finally got the balls to talk to him. Knowing Jeff, he wouldn't have a lot to say, but his thick, tense silence would speak volumes.

When my plane landed, I had no one to pick me up. My mom lived in Flint, and we didn't get along. Jeff was part of my problems. The only choice left was Jamie. She showed up an hour and a half after I landed. I spent most of that time in a little bar, nursing a margarita and attempting to get a hold of my crazed emotions.

A part of me wanted to fly straight back to New York and punch Chase in the face. Another part wanted to give him a chance to explain. The third part of me wanted to run to Jeff and beg him to take me back. The fourth and, at that moment, the strongest part wanted to just forget both of them and bury my head in the sand.

Being pulled in four different directions emotionally is confusing and exhausting.

Jamie is really my only friend aside from Jeff. We've been roommates for nearly three years now, through two moves, several tragedies between the two of us, and innumerable break-ups, mostly on her end. She's a serial dater. She's the girl who has a new boyfriend every few weeks or months, but nothing is ever serious and she rarely ever gets truly emotional about breaking up with them. They're just hook-ups for her. I've never understood how she can go from guy to guy and not get attached. She claims they're fun for a while, but then she gets bored.

I'm not that type. I get attached. My thing with Chase should've been just a fling: fun for a while, then over. I shouldn't have been devastated when I found him in the alley with those girls. But I was. I felt betrayed and confused. And now, with a couple thousand miles between us, I realized I'd been stupid to think it ever could have been anything for Chase but what it was: a fun distraction. He talked a good game, made it seem like he really cared, like it meant something to him.

He was a rock star, and I was his flavor of the week.

I'd turned my phone on to call Jamie, after having turned it off in the airport so I wouldn't hear Chase's deluge of texts and calls trying to explain away his bullshit.

I scrolled through the missed call log: he'd called me eighteen times and left ten voicemails. I dialed my voicemail and started hitting the "seven" button: delete, delete, delete. I couldn't help hearing snatches of the messages:

"Anna, I know what you think you saw, but please, give me a chance to explain. It wasn't—"

Delete.

"Goddammit, Anna. You have to listen. Please answer the phone—"

Delete.

"Seriously, Anna. It's not what you thought. I swear—"

Delete.

"Anna, for fuck's sake—"

Delete.

"Anna, this is the last message I'll leave. You're not answering, and your phone's going straight to voicemail, so I'm guessing you're not even listening to these. You're making a mistake. This is all a misunderstanding. I didn't do anything with those girls. They threw themselves at me. I would never...I care about you...I lo—"

Delete.

Oh, yeah. He went there.

I was shaking with rage, standing at the curb waiting for Jamie's battered blue Buick LeSabre. He wanted me to believe it was all them? Horseshit. I wanted to throw the phone across the road and watch it smash, but I didn't, because I couldn't afford a new one. I deleted his twenty-three texts unread.

I had one message that I hadn't read yet. I'd seen the unread mail icon but ignored it while I was in New York. It wasn't a text; it was an email. From Jeff.

Anna:

I don't blame you for going to New York. Seriously. I get it. I'm not saying I like it, or that I'm not hurt, but I get it. Just be smart, okay? Don't let yourself get hurt. I don't know this Chase fella, and I'm not going to butt into your business, when you clearly don't want me in it. Just be careful. I don't know what I'm trying to say.

Here's my point. I'm your friend, aside from anything else. If things don't work out for you, or if they do, I'll still be your friend. I can't guarantee anything else, but at the very least, I'll be your friend. And your business partner.

I guess that's all.

Jeff

It was dated the day I left for New York. It made my eyes burn. I'd gotten my crying jag under control, but reading Jeff's email made tears prick my red and burning eyes all over again.

Stupid Jeff. He should be pissed off. He should be too angry to want to see me ever again. He had to know why I went to New York, what I was doing with Chase. He'd admitted in his roundabout Jeff sort of way to being hurt; for him to admit that in writing meant he was very deeply wounded.

But he was still willing to be my friend and business partner? How the hell was that possible? If he'd done that to me, I'd never have spoken to him again. He was a better person than I, apparently.

The racketing roar of a car without a muffler disrupted my thoughts. Jamie's LeSabre pulled up next to me. The trunk popped, and Jamie hopped out. She was a few inches shorter than me, making her not quite five-seven, and she was built a bit more willowy and svelte than me, which always made me jealous. She wore most of her weight in her hips and breasts, which were more than ample. She often talked, only halfway joking, about getting a breast reduction, if only to save her some back pain. She was a natural redhead, pure Irish orange-copper locks falling past her shoulders in absurdly perfect waves, and pale cornflower-blue eyes, freckles, the whole nine yards.

When I said she was willowy and svelte, that was relatively speaking. She's still what most people would call "plus-size." Which is why she's my best friend. We understand each other. We tell each other, when life hands us pain due to the fact that we're not diet-obsessed stick figures, that God just gave us an extra portion of awesomeness. And then we watch *Breakfast at Tiffany's* and share a pint of Ben and Jerry's, washed down with a bottle of wine.

In this moment, with Chase in New York and Jeff shoved aside until I had the courage to face him, Jamie was the only person I could stomach.

She was my only real family, and the one person who'd understand what I needed in that moment: cupcakes and alcohol.

She had a six-pack of Tim Horton's muffins (three left) and a grande skinny mocha waiting for me. Yeah, she's that kind of friend.

"I honestly didn't expect you to come back," Jamie said as I slid into the passenger seat.

The engine roared, and I held onto my mocha with one hand and the oh-shit bar with the other. Jamie is an...exuberant driver.

"I'm not sure I did, either," I answered, unwrapping the low-fat blueberry muffin.

"So what the hell happened?"

I ate the muffin and thought about how much to tell Jamie.

"Everything happened," I answered, after a few bites. "He took me backstage for a couple shows, which was awesome. We hung out a lot, which was also awesome. And then I caught him with some groupies in an alley. Which was not awesome."

Jamie frowned at my Spark's Notes version of events. "Come on, Anna. Spill. Don't be selfish with the gossip."

I rolled my eyes. "It's not gossip, Jay. It's my life. And it hurt."

Jamie backhanded my shoulder. "I know. We can get to the hurt later. For now, tell me the good stuff. Is he good in bed?"

I realized I hadn't really talked to Jamie about Chase at all since I'd met him.

"He's...god, where do I start?" I closed my eyes and grabbed the oh-shit bar as Jamie merged onto the freeway. When we were cruising at a relatively tame eighty-five, I started talking again. "Chase is a rock star in every sense of the word. Nothing I've ever done, with anyone, can even remotely compare to Chase in bed."

"Is he big?"

I choked on my muffin. "I didn't exactly measure, Jay, but yes, he is. And that's all I'll say. A girl's gotta have some secrets."

"Not from your best friend, you don't. But seriously, if he's that good, why come home?"

"I told you, I found him porking some chicks in an alley."

Jamie frowned. "Are you sure? If he's as hot as you claim, which I wouldn't know because you wouldn't introduce me, then girls would be throwing themselves at him, right? So maybe it wasn't how it looked. Did you give him a chance to explain?"

I ignored the niggling worm of doubt in my gut. "I didn't need to. I know what I saw."

Jamie looked at me, and it wasn't a look I liked. "So you just left? You just got on a plane and left, without listening to anything he had to say? Nothing?"

"Whose side are you on?" I suddenly wasn't interested in the other two muffins.

"I'm on yours, which is why I'm pissed off. You should have at least given him a chance." She narrowed her eyes at me, as if coming to a realization. "You ran because you like him. Right? It wasn't just the girls. That was an excuse. You have feelings for him."

"Feelings" was a swear word in Jamie's dictionary. Feelings led to pain, which she'd had enough of in her life. Just like me.

"I flew to New York on a whim to see him, Jamie. Yes, I have feelings for him."

Jamie gave me an exasperated look. "No, dumbass. You like him, like him. Meaning, you're worried you're falling in love with him, so you bolted."

The guardrail out my window was suddenly interesting. "No. That's not it."

Jamie shrieked, "It is! You love him. But you're chicken."

I rounded on her, pissed off now. "And you wouldn't be? If you found yourself falling in love with a guy way out of your league, you'd be shitting yourself, too, and you know it."

"True. But I'd be honest about it."

"And I'm not?"

Jamie didn't answer right away, tongue poking out the side of her mouth as she focused on weaving around a train of slow-going semis. When I could breathe again, and she had decelerated down to ninety, she gave me a serious look.

"No, you're not. You ran without telling him what you were feeling. Let's just say, just for argument's sake, that you're wrong about what you saw. And let's say he invited you to New York because maybe, just maybe, he has feelings for you, too. And then some girls jumped him in the alley, and you walked out and saw something incriminating, and left without so much as a how-de-do. How would he feel, do you think?"

My stomach clenched. "Who the hell are you, and what did you do with my best friend? Because it sure as hell sounds like you're advocating a real relationship with actual feelings here."

Jamie kept her eyes on the road, both hands clenched on the steering wheel. I'd never seen Jamie use both hands to drive. She always had one hand on the gear shifter, even though her car was automatic.

"Listen, Anna. I know I'm like the all-time queen of humping and dumping guys. I act all 'fuck feelings' and whatever, and that's true enough. I mean, it's not an act. But, deep down, when I'm doing the walk of shame to my car at three a.m., I do wonder what it would be like to really have a guy care about me. Like, want me, and want me to stay over." She gave me long, sad look. "I find myself wondering what it would be like to have a guy want me for me, not just because I'm easy, you know?"

"You're not easy, Jay—"

"I am, too. I am and I like it that way. Usually. But sometimes, I wish a guy would see past the tits and ass. The problem is, I don't let them, because it keeps the ones who might feel something at bay."

"You've really thought about this, haven't you?"

She nodded, rubbing across her cheek with a forefinger. Almost like she was crying, which was absurd. Jamie didn't cry.

"Yeah, of course. More than I'd ever admit to." She looked at me, let me see the diamonds glittering in her eyes. "I'm just saying, Anna, if Chase was for real, then…I don't know. Maybe you should have given him a chance."

It was hard to breathe for a few minutes. This was the deepest Jamie had ever let me see into who she really was. I mean, best friends, yeah, but deepest, darkest, most vulnerable secrets? Not usually.

"It was more than that, Jay." I picked at the fraying seam threads of her leather seats between my thighs. "I was confused."

"Confused? By what?"

"I think…I thought—"

"Spit it out, sister."

I took a deep breath and said what I'd been worried about for days. "I have feelings for Jeff, too."

"Shit on a shingle."

"Exactly." I pulled my hair out of the ponytail and ran my fingers through it. "I think they both have feelings for me, too. Or...did. After leaving Jeff like I did, I'm not sure where that stands. I really made a mess of things."

Jamie took my hand and squeezed it. "When you said no one could compare to Chase in bed..."

I shook my head. "They're completely different. I don't know how to think about them at the same time, you know? It's like trying to compare apples and cheese."

"Apples and cheese go great together..." Jamie winked at me.

"Oh, hell no."

"It's never even crossed your mind?"

"Both of them at the same time?" I looked at her with horror. "You should know me better than that. I would never, could never, with anyone. Much less two men I care for. I don't know how you could do that and then look at either guy the same way again."

"You'd be surprised," Jamie said.

"You mean, you—?"

"ANYWAY," Jamie said, a little too loudly, "if they're so different, then it should make it easier to decide, right? Just pick the one you like sleeping with more."

"I wish it was that simple," I said. "I don't know how to explain it. Chase is wild. We do crazy things. Like…whoa. But Jeff? Jeff is just slow and sweet and…."

Jamie raised an eyebrow. "Keep going. Tell me about wild and crazy."

"Like, in the bathroom of a bar. And in a changing room. Tied up. Blindfolded."

"No fucking way. Blindfolded?" Jamie grinned at me, incredulous. "I've done it in public places before, no problem. Fun and risky, but whatever. Old news, and gets uncomfortable, just like in cars. But, seriously? Blindfolded? Tied up? Tell me about it! What's it like?"

"Intense. Tied up requires serious trust. Even if you have a safeword, you have to trust him to listen if you use it. But god, is it hot. You have no idea what he's going to do next. You can't do anything back to him, you just have to lie there and let him do whatever he wants. He can make you wait for hours, if he has the patience. Blindfolded is different. Without sight, everything else is more vivid. Smell, hearing, touch…"

Jamie moaned and slid down low in her seat. "Okay, enough. You're making me horny and jealous. I don't have anyone I trust enough to do that with. Sounds incredible."

"It is."

"Soooo….what's the problem?"

"I didn't say there was a problem. I had no idea it could be like that. Just no clue."

"So, then, what about Jeff?"

I didn't answer for a long time. "With Jeff it's not as…exciting. Like, not as wild and unpredict-able. But he's amazing, in his own way. It doesn't need to be crazy to be just completely satisfying, on a soul-deep level. He takes me places, emotionally and physically, where I didn't know two people could go together. It's just a totally different expe-rience. I'm not sure I can describe it."

Jamie was silent for awhile. "So you have two amazing guys. Both have feelings for you, and you have feelings for both of them, but they're totally different."

"Basically. And I've messed it up with both of them. I mean, I'm not sold on Chase being inno-cent. But if he is…?"

"All you can do is make the best choice you can and try to fix things with whichever one you pick."

"It's a shitty choice. Whatever I do, someone gets hurt. And with Jeff, I'm not sure there's any picking left. I ran to New York to fuck Chase less than forty-eight hours after sleeping with Jeff. How does that not make me some kind of slut?"

"Beating yourself up won't help. And it wasn't like that."

"No? How was it then? I got a letter with a plane ticket. All the letter said was, 'I need to see you.' And I just went. Left Jeff just when things were getting interesting.

"By which you mean an emotional connection was starting?" Jamie said.

"Yeah, basically. I mean, with Jeff, I think there always was. I've known him for so long, and we know each other on a completely different level, you know? Jeff was my business partner, and besides you, my best and only other friend. Sleeping with him didn't change our friendship, really. It just... deepened it. At least, until I left. I don't know if there's anything left to go back to. He did send me an email saying he'd still be my friend, but I don't know how far that goes. I really hurt him."

Jamie bit her lip. "He said that? In an email?"

I nodded. "Yeah. He sent it just after I left Detroit. I didn't see it until just now, though. I never really used my phone in New York."

"If he said that, that he's still your friend, then I'm willing to bet he's still in love with you. He'd give you a chance. I know Jeff well enough to know he'd probably forgive you."

"I'm not sure. And should he?"

"Of course he should. People do shitty things. You forgive them and move on."

"Is that why we never let anyone in? Because we forgive and move on?"

Jamie laughed. "Well, people that aren't us. We're messed up."

We rode in companionable silence for a while. We were nearly back to our apartment when Jamie spoke up again.

"So what are you going to do?"

I shrugged. "I don't know. I really don't."

"Well, don't wait too long. The longer you put it off, the harder it'll get."

"Yeah, you're right." I agreed with her out loud, but inside, I was wondering if maybe I should just pretend nothing had happened. Get a job somewhere else, stop DJing so I didn't have to see Jeff, and move on with my life, without either man.

It was the coward's way out, but it would be easier than dealing with Jeff's hurt eyes and hard silence.

I hid in my room for two days, then took some independent DJing jobs. I drank too much with Jamie. I ignored the waning amount of texts from Chase.

Basically, I tried to pretend nothing had happened, or would happen. I don't know if Jeff even knew I was back in Detroit.

With every passing day I wanted more and more to see Jeff, if only to apologize. Being here, in my apartment, passing places where I'd DJed with him, places where we'd had dinner before work… it all made me realize what I'd given up with him.

A week passed. Jamie held her tongue until I was halfway through the second week.

"Anna, you're being a coward and an idiot," she told me over our second bottle of two-buck Chuck. "If you don't woman up and do something besides avoid the situation, we're gonna be fighting. For real."

"I can't, Jay. I don't know what to do."

"Not doing anything isn't an option. You're better than this. If you don't want to be with either of them, fine. I think that's stupid, but it's your choice. If you have two men in love with you, you *have* to pick one of them, I'd think. It's hard enough to get *one* guy to feel something for you besides 'I want to fuck you.'" Jamie frowned at me in irritation. "Girl, I'm telling you as your friend, if you don't do *something*, you're gonna wake up one day and realize you made the biggest mistake of your life."

Her eyes welled up and she looked away, downed her glass of chardonnay. I suspected she was speaking from experience, but this seemed to be deeper than we'd gone. We'd always been "have a good time and don't talk about the past" kind of friends.

"What was his name?" I asked.

Jamie didn't answer for a long time. When she did, her voice was barely above a whisper. "Brian. We met a few months after I graduated from high school. My brother had just gone to jail. He'd gotten caught after a heroin-induced series of B and E's. Mom was high all the time, Dad was off with one of his hooker girlfriends. I had no one. No one came to my graduation, no one cared that I was valedictorian, despite not having parents who gave a shit. I'd known Brian all through high school, but in an opposite sides of the same circle of friends kind of way. Then, one day, I was out on the tracks, smoking down, feeling sorry for myself, wondering what the hell my life meant. Brian showed up, just swaggering down the tracks. Long metal-band hair, all-black clothes, skin-tight jeans and combat boots and spiked bracelets, the whole bit. He saw me smoking, sat down next to me, and we shared the J together. Didn't talk until it was gone.

"He...he got me. Had a similar home situation, and we just kind of talked about it enough to realize we were like the same person, you know? I didn't feel as alone, suddenly. He turned into my best friend. My only friend. We were inseparable after that. I think I saw him every single day for, like, a year. It was just friendship at first. Then one day we got really high and split a forty. He had his own place with a buddy who was twenty-one, bought beer all the time. We lay in Brian's bed, smoking and drinking.

"I don't even remember how it happened. One second we were just blazing and talking and whatever, and then we were kissing and our clothes were off, and…it just happened. You know, I always call bullshit when people say, 'oh it was accident, it just happened.' And most of the time, it is bullshit. It was a choice, and you just chose not to stop it, because really, you wanted it, and the consequences didn't seem so bad in that moment. But that night, with Brian, it really did just happen. I don't remember there ever being any sexual tension, or flirting, or whatever. It just…happened. I remember it all. Every sweet, incredible moment is burned into my brain forever.

"It freaked me the fuck out. I've got damage, Anna. You know that. I've got guy issues, and it all goes back to my dad not loving me or whatever. I've had that shit psychoanalyzed dozens of times. Knowing why I've got issues doesn't make 'em go away. Well, Brian had mommy issues like I've got daddy issues, and together, it just made things impossible. He wanted to work it out, give it a try. We got each other, on a fundamental, emotional level. We didn't have to explain our walls and hot-button issues. And the sex was great. After that first time, we couldn't stop, you know? We just kept fucking every chance we got. But it was never any deeper than that, as in we never talked about what our relationship was, or about our feelings. Well, when he finally confronted me on the issue, told me we had to either talk it out or stop seeing each other...I bolted.

"He chased after me for weeks. Called me, hunted me down wherever I went, told me he loved me, wrote me songs. I pushed him away. Finally he took the hint and left me alone. Forever. And now, every day, I realize what a mistake I made. I should have let him love me, should've tried, shouldn't have been such a goddamned coward. It's too late, though. I tried. I looked for him, and I actually found him, but he'd gotten engaged to this great girl, and he was happy and just looked at me all sad, like, 'Too late, baby. Your loss.'"

Jamie had never talked about herself that much at once in all the time I've known her. She stood up and left, went into the bathroom and stayed there for a long time. Crying, probably. Getting it out in private.

When she came back, her eyes were red but she was back to normal. "Anyway, all that with Brian is the reason I am like I am. My therapist used to tell me the reason I go through guys like I do is because I'm looking for Brian, or someone like him."

"Is that why?" I asked.

She nodded. "Pretty much. I mean, do I look at every guy I go out with and ask myself if he's like Brian, or compare them to see if he matches up to Brian? No, not consciously. But I think down deep, subconsciously or whatever, I dismiss the guy before I've given him a chance just because he's not Brian and never will be. The problem is, Brian is gone. No one will ever be him. Someday I'm going to have to let go of him and my idea of a guy based on him. I think maybe I keep hoping some man will come along and just sweep me away, but so far, it hasn't happened, and I'm starting to wonder if it ever will."

"Let me ask you something, Jay. If a guy did come along who was somehow just different from all the others, would you let him sweep you away? Because so far, in my experience, it's not that easy. Getting swept away is scary, in reality. It's not all love stories and fairy tales." I looked at her over the rim of my wine glass. "You don't know what's happening, and everything you feel is freaking intense as hell, and nothing makes any sense and it's just... scary. It's not like, oh, hey, hot guy who likes me, let's go live happily ever-fucking-after. When you're as damaged as we are, a guy tries to sweep you away and you're like oh, hell no, I'm running. Screw this. I'm gonna go back to what's familiar."

Jamie nodded. "Yeah, that sounds about right." She smiled at me. "So if you've got that much figured out, then why haven't you done anything about Jeff or Chase?"

"Because I'm scared shitless, that's why." I laughed. "Avoiding them both is easier than being rejected. I hurt them, and now I don't have the guts to ask for forgiveness."

Jamie frowned, pointed at me with the index finger wrapped around her wine glass. "Well, woman the hell up, *chica*. You've fought off guys in bars, broken cue sticks and beer bottles over the heads of drunk assholes, and been through more insane shit than most guys I know and come through fine. Well, mostly fine. The point is, don't let this own you, girl. I'm serious. If you let this go, we'll be for real fighting. Don't be an idiot. Find Jeff and apologize and beg him, on your hands and knees, to take you back. Or fly to New York and get Chase to take you back. Something. Anything. Get them both here and have a threesome. Don't just sit around with your head up your ass. That's the only wrong choice in this situation."

She didn't give me a chance to respond. She downed her wine and wove her way unsteadily into her bedroom.

"I'm right, Anna, and you know it. Get off your ass. Right now."

"I'm drunk right now," I pointed out.

"Well, tomorrow, then. Drunk is never the right time to make major life decisions. Talk about major life decisions, yes. Do something about them? Not s'much. G'night, Anna."

"Night." I watched her flop onto her bed and start snoring immediately.

I've always envied her ability to go right to sleep. It always takes me a while, even drunk. I finished my wine, set her glass and mine by the sink, turned off the lights and shut Jamie's door. Alone, the silence was deafening. I heard Jamie's words in my head, rolling over and over: *Do something, anything. Get off your ass, girl.*

I lay down in bed and stared at the ceiling, thinking.

Enough running, Anna. No more cowardice.

I told myself I was going to call Jeff in the morning. Better yet, go to his house. Face him in person.

Oh, hell.

Jeff's Yukon was in his driveway, his front door was open, and I could see him through the storm door, sitting at the kitchen table in front of his laptop. My stomach was in my throat, my heart pounding in my chest like a high school drum line.

I was in my car, willing myself to get out. It wasn't working. My feet were planted to the floorboard, my ass rooted to the ripped cloth seat. My eyes were already burning, my throat thick, my hands trembling.

I had no idea what I was going to say.

Jeff's back was to me and he had earbuds in, so he didn't see me pull up in his driveway or hear my car rattle down the street. He was oblivious.

Would he slam the door in my face? Would he lead me inside and tell me he forgave me?

I forced myself out of the car. Took a step. Another. A third, and then I was at the door, the glass pane rattling under my trembling knuckles. Jeff looked over his shoulder, the pen in his mouth dropping to the floor.

He pulled the earbuds out of his ears and tossed them aside, closed the laptop, and moved across the small living room. He stopped in front of the door, his features schooled into neutrality. No anger showed, no sadness or condemnation. Blank.

After an eternity, he opened the door, but he didn't let me in. He stepped out onto the concrete slab that was his front porch. My eyes were blurry and stinging for some reason. I wasn't crying, though. Really.

Okay, so maybe I was, a little.

A long, fraught silence hung between us.

"Jeff, I—I'm sorry. I just wanted to stop by and say that I'm back in Detroit, and—I don't know." I couldn't look at him. "That's it, I guess."

He hadn't said anything yet, hadn't even changed his blank expression. I turned to leave, heart heavy and cracking.

I felt his hand wrap around my elbow. "Anna, wait." I tried not to let hope blossom too fully in my chest. "Why don't you come in and have some coffee?"

It was two in the afternoon, but for Jeff, coffee was an all-day thing. Leftover habit from the Army, I guess. I nodded and followed Jeff inside. I'd only been gone a few days, but it felt like longer. It felt like a lifetime. I realized, as I watched his broad back retreat into the kitchen, how very much I'd missed him. Had going to New York been the worst mistake of my life? It was hard not to think so, in light of my feelings of Chase's betrayal, whether he was guilty or not.

I sat down at the little round table, remembering breakfast here with Jeff, after what had been one of the best nights of my life. It hadn't been wild or acrobatic or daring, just satisfying on an emotional level. It was companionship.

I'd left it all behind for a few days of fun that hadn't panned out into more. And what if it had? What if I'd just stayed in New York with Chase? He'd be a huge rock star someday soon, traveling the world, playing shows in exotic locations. It was just a matter of time. Would I have gone with him? Stood backstage and watched every show every day for months on end? Sat in hotel rooms, waiting for him to get back? Attended insane after-parties like the one in New York? Would any of that have fulfilled me? Would he have been faithful all that time?

There were too many questions pounding in my head, and Jeff was sitting across from me, a huge mug with the U.S. Army logo stamped on it held in both of his hard, calloused hands.

"New York didn't work out for you, huh?" Jeff asked.

I shook my head. "I don't want to talk about New York."

Jeff's eyes narrowed. "He hurt you."

A short, tense silence, in which I tried to keep my feelings bottled up inside where they belonged. I couldn't just dump it all on Jeff.

"I said I don't want to talk about New York. I came to apologize for hurting you, and that's it. I—I didn't mean to hurt you. That doesn't help, I guess, but I had to say it." I sipped my coffee to buy time to think, burning my tongue. "I got your email when I got back in to Detroit. I don't know how you can say you're still my friend after the way I—after I—"

Jeff interrupted. "Anna, you'll always be my friend. You can't hurt me bad enough to kill that. I care about you. No matter what."

"You're a better person than I am," I said. "I'm not sure I could do the same, if the situations were reversed."

"I don't buy that," Jeff said. "You're a good person."

"No, I'm not. I wouldn't have left if I was."

"Well..." Jeff seemed conflicted. "You did leave. It did hurt. But does that make you a bad person? That's not for me to judge."

"This is a confusing conversation. I just came to apologize. I'm not...I'm not trying to get—to ask you to..." I couldn't get the words out.

I stood up and walked to the sliding glass door, watching a robin hop across Jeff's backyard. Jeff was making me even more mixed up inside. He seemed both deeply hurt and impossibly under-standing. I didn't know how to deal with either one, much less both at once.

"To what?" Jeff said. "You're not asking me to what? Spit it out."

I shook my head. "No. It's stupid to think of it, and not gonna happen. I don't deserve it, and I don't even know if I want it."

"Say it."

"No." I felt Jeff coming up behind me, standing an inch away, his body heat radiating into me, not touching me, his breath ruffling my hair. "Don't, Jeff. I apologized, and now I'm leaving."

"You didn't apologize," Jeff said. "Just told me you were sorry. That's not an apology."

I turned around, angry now. "You want me to say the words? Fine. Jeff, I apologize for hurt-ing you. Please forgive me." The words started out angry, irritated, but ended up as a cracked-voice sob.

Jeff's hands clutched my shoulders, held me at arm's length. "I forgive you, Anna." His dark eyes pierced into mine, a welter of emotion in his gaze.

"You shouldn't."

He laughed. "Of course I should. Friends forgive each other."

"Okay. So now what?"

"You tell me."

"It's not that easy," I said. "You can't just say 'I forgive you' and have everything go back to the way it was."

"Of course not," Jeff said. "But it's a start."

Jeff sat down at the table again and sipped his coffee. I joined him, and we drank in silence.

"What happened?" Jeff asked.

"You don't want to know."

"Sure I do. You're my friend. Something happened to rile you up and send you back to Detroit."

"Jeff, you really don't want to know. We're more than friends, and you know it. At least, we were. I don't know what we are now, but you don't want to know about New York."

"Don't tell me what I want," Jeff growled, anger finally showing in his voice. "We were more than friends. We still are. Now tell me what the fuck happened in New York."

"What do you want to know?" I felt myself on the verge of exploding, and I couldn't stop it. "Do you want to hear that Chase and I fucked like bunnies? That it was crazy and wild and I never wanted to stop? Or do you want to hear that even when I was with him I couldn't stop thinking about you? That I felt guilty with him because it felt like cheating on you? Is that what you want?"

"Anna, I—"

"Or would you like me to get more detailed? Do you want a play-by-play description of positions? Is that it? What do you want, Jeff? You can't honestly still want me after this, can you? What was it you said before we ever hooked up? Oh, yeah, I remember. You said you didn't want Chase's sloppy seconds. Well, I've got news for you, Jeff. That's what you'll be getting. Chase's really sloppy fucking seconds."

Jeff's eyes wavered, angry, hurt, confused, and still pinning me to the wall with impossible understanding. "Anna, now hold on, I already told you, I didn't mean that—"

I didn't let him finish yet again. "You want to know what happened? Why I came back? I found Chase in an alley after his show with a couple of girls all over him. I bolted. I didn't give him a chance to explain. I just left. I was on a flight home within two hours. It just made me so mad. It may not have been what I thought it was, because girls have a tendency of throwing themselves at Chase." I looked away. "Just like I did."

"Fuck," Jeff sighed. "The way I saw it, he threw himself at you. Granted, I didn't see it all, but that's the impression I got. He didn't seem like your type, to be honest."

"My type?"

"Yeah, I mean, he's all pretty boy rock star or whatever, and I've never seen you go after guys like that."

"Because I never thought I was enough for a guy like him."

"Damn it, Anna. You're beautiful. I know you have a hard time believing that, or seeing it in yourself, but it's true." Jeff touched my jaw, turning my gaze back to his. "I see it, Anna. You were always enough for me."

"Even after?"

"Yes. I'm not saying I'm not hurt and pissed off at you. I am. What I'm saying is, I'd be willing to try, if you were. If you want to give Chase another chance, then I guess that's your choice. I wouldn't, personally. I mean, even if it wasn't like you thought, and he wasn't really doing anything, he'd end up doing it one day. No guy can have women throw themselves at him like that and not give in sometime."

I didn't know what to say. Was he serious?

"Jeff, I—I don't know."

"You don't have to know right now," Jeff said. "Hell, I'm not even sure. I know I care about you. I know I'm sorry you got hurt. I know I've really missed you."

"Do you feel like I betrayed you?"

Jeff sighed. "Yeah, kinda." He refilled his coffee and spoke without looking at me while doctoring it. "I felt like we had a damn good thing going, and it could've been more, could've been even better. But then that pretty boy sends you one stupid letter and you run off to him without a second thought."

He sat down and looked at me. "Listen, I do understand. It was one of those things where you would've spent your whole life wondering 'what if.' You had to find out. Now you know, and you can move on."

"You're amazing, Jeff. I don't know what to say." I couldn't believe he was even giving me the time of day.

"I care about you. I'm not saying I'll trust you all the way again right off the bat. We'd have to take things slow for a while, because I am still a bit sore, you know? But you're back, and I...I just can't seem to picture my life without you in it, somehow."

I couldn't help crying at that. It was quiet tears, slow and burning down my face.

"Don't cry, Anna. You're gonna be fine. We'll be fine. One day at a time, okay?"

"I've been back for almost two weeks, you know that? I've spent every moment wondering what you'd say, how you'd react, thinking you'd be so mad."

"What, you think I'd yell at you? Scream and call you names?" Jeff seemed almost insulted by the thought.

"Well, I don't know! All I knew was I'd hurt you, and I didn't deserve—"

"Forget the talk about deserving. We are who we are. People who really love us will do so even when we hurt them."

"So you love?"

"Let's go get something to eat," Jeff interrupted. "I'm hungry."

It was awkward at first. We drove in Jeff's truck, a tense silence between us. Neither of us knew what we were, where we really stood. We hadn't settled anything, really. We'd just sort of... stopped talking about it. What else was there to say, really, though? Either things would work out, or they wouldn't. No amount of talking would get us past what had happened.

The funny thing was, I realized as we sat down together at Max and Erma's, we'd both just kind of assumed we'd try to...not pick up where we'd left off, but move on, be together in some way.

Jeff didn't bring up New York or Chase again. He talked about some interesting DJ gigs he'd done, did a few funny impressions of a drunk guy trying to sing "Brown-Eyed Girl," which was a song he hated, even when done by Van Morrison, and even more so when butchered by some wasted bar patron.

We'd always been comfortable together, an easy come-and-go to our conversations, silence that could stretch out for long periods of time without either of us needing to fill it with aimless chatter. At first, things were stilted, hesitant, and difficult. Awkward at best. But by the time we were done with our burgers and were sharing a brownie sundae, we were finding our old rhythms, our previous comfort.

Once again I was struck by how long it had seemed since we'd been apart. So much had changed. I had changed, somehow. I didn't see Jeff as a given commodity. That's really the truth of it. Jeff had been a consistent part of my life for so long that I had taken him for granted, assumed he'd be there no matter what. And then I left for New York on a whim, and somewhere along the way I realized he might not always be there, that maybe I'd pushed him away.

The thought of Jeff not being in my life, of not having his quiet, steady presence to rely on, scared me. He belonged in my life. I couldn't fathom working a gig without him to help set up. Couldn't fathom waking up and not being able to call him, or have lunch with him.

He was giving me another chance, and I vowed to not mess it up.

A little over two and a half weeks passed in which Jeff and I spent a lot of time together, as just friends—albeit friends with sexual chemistry sparking at every moment, in everything we did. Every conversation was rife with innuendo. Every touch threatened to ignite an inferno between us.

The breaking point came during a shift DJing at a Mexican place in Lake Orion two weeks later. We set up, ran through the first set without a problem. Some good singers did their numbers, and of course, as the night went on, some drunks did the usual murder to "Sweet Home Alabama" and "Margaritaville."

We took our break, ran a few more numbers, and then, as the fill music was playing between numbers, a guy maybe thirty-five or so sidled up to Jeff and me. He was tall, with brown hair and a goatee, a western-style shirt with pearl snap buttons and pointed breast pockets, a huge belt buckle, and cowboy boots, complete with a Stetson. His wife was sitting at a round high-top table, similarly decked out, but with jean skirt.

The gentleman leaned an elbow on the mixing board and addressed Jeff. "Can I make a special request?"

"Sure," Jeff said, setting a pencil and request slip down in front of the man and pointing at the songbook. "We've got plenty of country songs to choose from."

"Hell, no. I don't want to sing, and you don't want me to. I can guaran-damn-tee you that. If I get started, I'll clear the place in three bars flat."

"Well, then, what can I do for you?" Jeff asked.

"I want you and the lady here," he said, pointing at me, "to sing a song together. It's my wife and I's tenth anniversary today, and we'd sure appreciate hearing our favorite song."

My wife's and my, I mentally corrected, but didn't say out loud.

"Well, if we know it, we'll sing it," Jeff said.

"We'd like to hear 'Let's Make Love' by Tim McGraw and Faith Hill."

Jeff cast a glance at me. We knew that song. We'd listened to it just the other day, trundling down a narrow dirt track road in the middle of Milford, cruising and listening to music. The harmony fit our voices perfectly, and then, in the car, it had been hard enough to ignore the lyrics and keep driving.

Performing it together would be...intense.

"We know it," Jeff answered. "We'll sing it. And congratulations. Ten years together. That's really awesome."

"It takes a lot of hard work, a lot of compromise, and a lot of forgiveness," the man said, clapping Jeff on the shoulder. "If you love her, show her. That's the real trick. It takes a real man to let his feelings show to his wife."

Jeff just nodded and sent the man on his way back to his table. He hopped onto the high chair and flung his arm around his wife's shoulders, nuzzling her neck and whispering something in her ear that made her giggle and swat him on the arm.

Tapping a few commands into his laptop, Jeff brought up the song track and lyrics. We'd spent a lot of time over the last few weeks converting all our old CDs to digital tracks, so now we just had one laptop as opposed to several huge binders of discs. Jeff handed me one of the cordless mics, and we stepped out onto the stage together as the opening strains of the song came up.

In my mind, I see the music video: black and white images, a lovely blonde woman and a rugged, handsome man in a cowboy hat and duster dancing in front of the Eiffel Tower. The chemistry between the pair, as they dance together and begin singing, is clearly not acted, or performed, but real and genuine. It makes the lyrics of the song that much more powerful.

Jeff's clear tenor starts in, a bit low for his register but on key and...god, he's never sounded better. His eyes fix on mine, and his hand reaches for me. Sparks fly as his palm brushes across mine, our fingers tangle, and he turns to face me, no need for the prompter or the crowd, gone silent now, caught up in the moment, as I am. My part comes, and I hear my voice rising up, pitch-perfect and clarion clear, and I know I'm on, I can feel the rightness in my bones, I can feel the music boiling in my blood and the buzz of adrenaline from performing, even for the hundred or so bar patrons. None of that matters, though, because it's the song, the lyrics, the moment. Jeff is clutching my hand, pulling me close, our bodies almost touching, our eyes locked as if connected. I couldn't look away from him if I wanted to. This is beyond chemistry, beyond spark.

Something is happening, in this moment, as I sing, as he sings, as we harmonize, as the music coils around us like serpents of visible flame, burns through us like dulcet fire.

They say the eyes are the window to the soul; as we sing, those windows are flung open and our souls collide. It's the kind of moment you never forget. The song doesn't end, in my memory. It just keeps going, and we keep singing. Our hands are joined, we're singing from one mic, the crowd is stunned, eyes are glistening.

The couple who requested the song, the cowboy and his wife, they're dancing together in front of their table. No one else is dancing, or even moving at all. Even the bartenders and the servers are paused, trays of drinks set down, pints of beer half-filled. A few cooks are even peeking out from the doors of the kitchen. The couple dances, cheeks pressed together, heads inclined a little, bodies pressed close into a hold that's more embrace than anything else. They dance slowly, swaying in gradual circles. You can feel the love pouring between them, and you can't help but wonder what it must feel like to love someone that hard. How well must they know each other by now? Ten years of every single day? Ten years of conversation shared, secrets spilled, fears faced, and love made? They must be nearly one person by now, a single whole made from two inseparable halves.

Ten years is a long time to love someone. Your biological family is different, you know? They have to love you. Or, they're supposed to, but they don't always, which makes it even worse, I think. But to choose someone, one man, one woman, out of the thousands and millions of people in the world, all the different individuals you *could* love, *could* be with, you've chosen that *one* person, and you've stuck with them for an entire decade. You hear about people being married for twenty, forty, sixty years. I can't fathom that, not in any sense. Ten years I can imagine. I've known Jeff for six years. I can see us spending another ten together, if I don't fuck it up.

Our song, in reality, does end. The music fades away, and Jeff and I continue to hold hands. Our eyes are locked, mics held down by our sides. The crowd is still silent, as if waiting.

I'm waiting, too, I realize. I'm holding my breath, looking up at Jeff with his dark eyes glittering into mine.

He kisses me, a slow inevitability, lips touching in hesitant tenderness. His hand drifts up to my face, cups my cheek, thumb brushing my ear, and then the hand holding the mic is wrapping around my back and holding me closer, tighter, and the kiss is going deeper, and the crowd, silent, watching us kiss, seems to know better than to even breathe.

Time stopped for that kiss, I swear. Time was stopped for the whole song, and that kiss was part of it. When we broke apart, the crowd burst into frenzied cheering, clapping, whistling. The cowboy and his wife approached us, shook Jeff's hand, and gave me a hug.

"That was the best anniversary present we've ever gotten," the cowboy said. "I swear, y'all sounded just like Tim and Faith, if not better."

"Thanks," Jeff said. "Congratulations again."

"No reason for congratulations," the wife said. "It's just love."

The couple left then, but before they were out the door, the woman came back and leaned close to me. "That boy loves you, honey. Don't let him get away."

The same thought had crossed my mind.

We finished the shift, energy and tension sparking between us. Every time our fingers touched, every time our eyes met, I saw him in the shower, naked body heavy with muscle and dripping with rivulets of steaming water. I felt him above me in his wide, soft bed, dark eyes burning into mine as he moved, his rippling muscles pulsing his thick manhood into me.

It had been over a month since I left New York, and almost six weeks since that night in the hot tub. That was the one moment I saw in my mind, in my dreams, more than any other. Jeff, his solid bulk beneath me in the boiling water, our bodies moving in synchronized splendor, heat throbbing between us, fragments of our souls merging in the cool of the night and the spark of the stars and the thrum of our united passions.

I wanted him, so badly. We'd waited, through some kind of unspoken agreement, putting time between us and…all that. I didn't think I could wait any longer. Not now, not with the incredible performance we'd just shared, that song, those lyrics.

Jeff seemed to feel it, too. He got the equipment put away in record time, and we took our pay and left, not stopping for a drink or two like we usually did. The other gigs we'd done together in the past couple weeks, we'd had a couple of drinks, or gone to get some late night food. We hadn't gone back to either of our places.

Now, we stood by our cars, keys in hand, mere inches separating us.

"Thought maybe you'd come over for a bit," Jeff said, after a pregnant silence.

My lip curled in amusement. "Just for a bit?"

Jeff's eyes glinted his amusement. "Yeah. Just for a bit. I need my beauty rest, you know."

"Yeah, you sure do. Wouldn't want to keep you up too late, or tire you out."

"No, we wouldn't want that." Jeff pinched my chin gently between his thumb and forefinger, leaned in and kissed me.

It was delicate, gentle, a caress of the lips. The kiss communicated so much that he hadn't said in words. His slow and thorough devouring of my mouth and my tongue told me he'd forgiven me, he'd moved on and left the past behind us. His hand curling around my waist and pulling me against him told me he wanted me, told me he desired my body.

"Let's go," I said, "or we won't be going anywhere."

Jeff nodded and pecked me on the lips before getting into his Yukon. I think we made it back to his place in record time. I don't even remember the drive, honestly. I was so caught up in my thoughts of Jeff and what I wanted to do with him that I seemed to look up and find myself in his driveway.

He opened my car door, took my hand to help me out and to my feet. He didn't let go of my hand, even to unlock the front door. He reached to his left pocket with his right hand rather than let go, which was awkwardly funny enough that I laughed at him.

Inside, Jeff closed the door with his heel, then slowly turned to face me, taking my other hand in his.

"I said it once before, and I'll say it again: Don't play me, Anna. Not again. I can't take it again. Once I can forgive and forget. Not twice."

"I won't, Jeff, I promise. I'm here, and I'm not going anywhere."

"You promise?"

"I said so, didn't I?"

Jeff squeezed my hands, his eyes serious. "Say it again. Say, 'I promise I'll never leave you again, Jeff.'"

I took a deep breath. "I promise I'll never leave you again, Jeff."

My heart was hammering in my chest as I spoke the words. I felt like I'd crossed a line I could never uncross. I'd promised to never leave him. A quiet but fierce voice in my soul told me I'd just made a promise I could never, ever break. Jeff was the epitome of the strong, silent type. He didn't say much, but when he did, he meant it, and you listened. He didn't express his emotions much, but when he did, they were deep, rooted in his very identity. If I broke this promise to him, he wouldn't get over it. If I was to ever walk away from him, it'd be forever.

He was watching me carefully. Watching for hesitation, watching for regret, for some part of me being held back.

"I'm serious, Jeff. I won't."

"Better not." He was smiling now, inching closer, dark eyes vivid in the gloom of his unlit house.

I closed the gap between us, pressed my body up against his. He'd hugged me since I'd been back, but he hadn't held me. Now, he wrapped his arms around me, snugging me into the hollows of his body, my curves fitting into his angles as if we'd been cut from the same puzzle.

I pressed my cheek to his chest, heard and felt his heart thump-thumping, smelling the scent of Jeff—sweat, cologne, something else indefinable, something that was just Jeff, male and comforting—and feeling like I'd come home.

"You belong here," Jeff murmured.

He didn't mean his house, and I knew it.

"I'm home," I said.

My heart was expanding, ballooning, bursting. It hurt, in an odd, frightening way. It was a good thing, a feeling of belonging, of being protected, but it was scary. I knew I couldn't go back to the way I was before this moment. This was indelible, imprinted on me.

Neither of us had spoken the words, the three words that make things like this seem so permanent, but we didn't need to. It was there, writhing in the spaces between the other words, the pauses for breath when he dipped down to kiss me again, it was in the gap between his fingers as they at long last slipped under the hem of my shirt to brush my aching, waiting skin.

I mirrored his action, sliding my palms up his back, tracing the cords and ridges and planes of muscle. This felt like our first time, in a way. We were going slow, exploring, questing. His lips danced down to my chin, along my jaw to just beneath my ear, and I tipped my head back, eyes closed, as he continued to plant hot, moist kisses down my throat to the hollow at the base, just above my breastbone.

My palms carved around to press against the slabs of heavy muscle along his sides and stomach, up to his chest, to the hard little nubs of his nipples, and then his arms were above his head and his shirt was off, tossed aside. I was growing impatient, wanting more, wanting all of him now. An ache was starting deep in my core, throbbing between my thighs, spreading heat and the wetness of desire through my sex. Jeff's hands were everywhere now, pushing my shirt over my head and unclasping my bra as his mouth trailed between my breasts, tongue flicking each nipple in turn as the bra fell away.

"Take me to bed, Jeff," I whispered.

Both of us topless, Jeff led me to his room, left the light off so our only source of illumination was the silver wash from the gibbous moon and spattered, sparkling stars. We stood for a moment in the pale square of light from the window, looking at each other, not touching or speaking, only regarding, waiting for the other to move first.

Jeff only smiled at me, and stood waiting. I unbuttoned my pants, shimmied out of them, posed for Jeff in my panties, my weight on one leg, the other bent so only my toe touched the ground, crossed in front of my other leg. I crossed my arms across my chest, then slid my palms under my breasts, lifting them, pinching my nipples, watching Jeff's reaction.

His zipper bulged out as I toyed with my breasts, then grew even larger when I pushed my panties off and kicked them aside. Jeff still hadn't moved, so I continued touching myself. I ran my hands down my ribs, past my belly and to the mound of my aching pussy. Jeff's tongue ran along his lips, and now his fingers unbuttoned his jeans, and then paused. I dipped my middle finger between my labia, and Jeff unzipped his pants. I circled my clit slowly until a gasp escaped; Jeff kicked his jeans aside and hooked his thumbs under the elastic of his boxer-briefs. I put one hand to my breast and rolled a nipple between my fingers, swirling two fingers around my clit with the other hand. Now Jeff drew his boxers off, revealing his thick, rigid cock, straining erect and leaking pre-come, begging to be touched.

I was done with games, suddenly.

I pushed Jeff backward to the bed, followed him as he crawled back to lie on his back. He curled his hands around my hips, traced my curves, hefted the weight of my breasts, looking up at me with a frightening tenderness in his eyes along with the desire. His hands continued their upward journey, his rough palm sliding along my cheek, cupping there as he lifted up to kiss me, then slowly and carefully sliding my hair out of the elastic band of my ponytail. My blonde waves fell down around our faces, and now his other hand slipped down my belly and between my thighs as I knelt above him.

I moaned into his mouth as we kissed, his fingers working magic, spreading fire up from my pussy to the rest of my body, a climax rising before he'd even entered me. I reached between us with one hand to grasp his cock, our foreheads touching as I ran my fingers up and down his length. I rubbed his tip in circles with my thumb, slid down to the root and massaged his balls before caressing his length once more.

Jeff continued to circle my clit with a gentle finger, pushing me up and over into orgasm. I whimpered, collapsed on top of him.

"Take me now, Jeff, please."

I guided him into me, a vocal moan filling the room as he penetrated deep into me, filling me.

"Sweet Jesus, you feel so good," Jeff said, thrusting slowly. "You feel like heaven."

My lips were crushed against his breastbone as I lifted my hips and slid back down his hard length, my arms against his sides, my hands on his shoulders, only our hips moving. His hands rested on my ass, curled around the taut-flexed globes.

"I'm gonna come again," I moaned.

"Yes, come for me, Anna." Jeff pulled on my ass, lifting me up and letting me fall, his body thrusting against mine.

I sat up straight, balancing on top of him with my hands on my thighs, riding him hard, rolling my passion-slick slit onto his cock with a frenzy of sighs and shrieks. I came, holding myself upright with my palms planted on Jeff's chest.

Jeff's arms wrapped around me, pulled me down to him, and then we moved in a dizzy roll and he was above me, in me, all around me. I locked my legs around his waist and my arms around his neck, clung tight to him, pressed my quivering lips to his and rocked into him, felt his turgid cock pushing deep into me, huge and hard and wonderful.

Another orgasm washed through me, this one coming in waves, a crest of ecstasy thrilling through me with each thrust of his cock. He was close now, his rhythm growing frantic, his thrusts harder and deeper. I drove my hips against him to match his rhythm, to match the frenetic fury of his rising climax.

"Come with me, Jeff," I said. "Come hard."

Jeff's eyes flew open and met mine, his gaze blazing with intensity. He plunged hard into me, paused with our hips flush, then pulled out again. As he drove himself into me once more, he came, flooding me, his gasp of pleasure a low-voiced growl.

He arched his back and thrust again, wet heat shooting into me once more, and now his forehead bumped mine and his ragged breathing echoed loud in the silver-lit room.

"I love you, Anna." He whispered it into the silence between breaths, into the stillness between thrusts, into the space between heartbeats.

His eyes were on mine as he said it, our bodies merged, our essences mingling, united in the flush of climax.

Tears started in my eyes, burned as they trickled down my cheeks to drip past my jaw beneath my ear.

"I lo?" I choked back a sob. "I love you. God, I love you." Saying it felt like a release.

I did love him. I couldn't imagine ever leaving him, ever being without him. I felt like I'd spent all my life waiting for him, and just never knew it, couldn't see it, or understand that he was what I needed. He'd been there, too close to see.

We were still moving together, roiling in the silence of soughing breaths, my tamped-down sobs of weltering emotions punctuating the rhythm of our lovemaking.

This wasn't sex, wasn't fucking, wasn't even just shared pleasure. This was, finally, a true expression of joined emotions, and I knew I couldn't ever match this experience, not with anyone else, not for as long as I lived.

Jeff didn't wipe away my tears, didn't shush me, or tell me it was okay, or ask why I was crying. He just kissed me tenderly, whispered my name.

We lay side by side, facing each other, our eyes speaking a thousand words that didn't pass our lips.

We fell asleep, woke up in the early dawn spooning, his erection hard against my ass. I guided him in and we rocked like that, back to front, his hand on my hip, his breath on my shoulder, slow and unhurried and uncomplicatedly sensual. We came at the exact same moment, and when we did, our fingers tangled across my breast, over my pounding heart.

We slept again, woke up past noon, and showered together, making love yet again, standing up in his shower, just like the first time.

A few more days passed, just like that. We didn't leave each other's side for more than a few minutes. We made love constantly, and the words "I love you" came more easily.

One of the few times we were apart Jeff wouldn't tell me where he was going. He left around two in the afternoon and didn't come back until almost five, and wouldn't answer one question, just insisted that I wait and find out. His eyes shone with amusement, telling me I would probably enjoy the surprise, so I left off questioning him and went along with it.

He came home, his home—which I was starting to consider home as well—and told me to get changed, to put on a dress or skirt of some sort. He stood in the doorway of the bedroom, watching me change. I slipped off the stretchy yoga pants and cotton panties I'd been wearing, as well as the T-shirt and sports bra. I took my time picking my outfit, naked, waiting for Jeff to sidle up behind me and start something, but he didn't, just watched with a smile on his face.

I picked a knee-length skirt and a button-down shirt, and a matching set of red lace lingerie. I started to put on the panties, but Jeff spoke up from the doorway.

"Leave 'em off. Go commando. We're gonna be somewhere private, so no one'll know but me," he said.

I stared at him for a moment, considering. I never went anywhere without panties on. It was just...not something I did. I didn't know any girls who did go out without panties on. It seemed skanky, somehow. I'm sure there were girls out there who would go to the bar with a little skirt on and no panties, but that wasn't me. Jeff had promised we'd be in private, though, so I went along with it, slipping the skirt up over my hips and zipping it. It felt strange, like being naked.

When I was fully dressed and had done a little makeup, against Jeff's protestations that I didn't need it, we left, Jeff driving. We drove for almost an hour, going far out into the country. We eventually came to a wide, rolling grassy field, a huge spreading oak tree in the middle, casting long shadows in the golden light of early evening. Jeff pulled the truck to a stop on the side of the narrow, empty dirt road and parked. From his trunk he retrieved wicker picnic basket and a folded quilt.

"We're going on a picnic?" I asked.

"Yep. Never been on an actual, factual picnic like this before, so I thought it might be a fun change from dinner at a restaurant. 'Sides, it's a beautiful evening."

I stuck my hand through his arm as we walked together across the field toward the tree. "I've never been on a picnic like this, either," I said. "Whose property is this?"

"An Army buddy of mine. He owns several hundred acres, I think. Most of it is farmland, but this here is just an empty field he doesn't use for much of anything."

"Does he know we're here?"

"Nah, but he won't care. He never comes out this way. His crops are all closer to his house, 'bout a mile that way," Jeff said, pointing off to the east.

We reached the tree, spread the blanket under the canopy of its branches. Jeff had put together an impressive spread of food, sandwiches, potato salad, pasta salad, fruit salad, key lime pie, sparkling mineral water, and a bottle of expensive champagne. We ate leisurely, drinking the water. I wondered about the champagne, but didn't say anything.

When we were both full, Jeff packed the basket once more. Jeff lay on his back and pulled me into his embrace, holding me close, his hand stroking my back. He was wearing a white button-down, and I popped each button open until his torso was bare. I spent awhile tracing the contours of his chest before I moved on to his belt, unbuckling it, unclasping his pants, unzipping them. He was semi-erect, growing larger as I watched.

There was an oddly shaped bulge in the pocket of his pants. I dismissed it, though, eager to feel his flesh firming in my hands. I pushed his pants and boxers off, set them aside.

I climbed astride him, thankful now that he'd had me leave my panties off. I was already bare to him, completely clothed even as he speared into me, gasping and his eyes crossing, fluttering, closing.

My skirt billowed around our hips, covering his belly and the joining of our bodies. I wanted to feel the air and the sun on my skin, though. I led Jeff's hands to my buttons, and he undid them, brushed the fabric from my shoulders and stripped off my bra, rocking into me all the while. His hands brushed over my ribcage and caressed my breasts, squeezed them, and rolled my nipples in his fingers. He lifted up to take a taut peak into his mouth, nipped lightly, sending jolts of electricity through me. He was pounding up into me, our bodies gyrating in sync, fire blossoming between us, in the merged heat and sweat of our flesh. I rocked above him, rode him to climax, palms flat on his chest.

When I came, I screamed at the top of my lungs, shrieked his name. I'd always been fairly vocal during sex, and found it hard not to be. This was the first time I'd let myself go wild, totally uninhibited, and god...screaming that loud made me come even harder, turned Jeff into a primal beast beneath me, his fingers locked around my hips and driving me down onto him, harder and harder, his cock plunging up and lifting me clear off the ground, his roar of climax every bit as loud as mine. Hearing him bellow as he came inside me drove me to a new orgasm, and now our voices were raised together in the golden evening light.

I rode him, coming, until he softened within me, and then I collapsed on top of him, still shuddering with aftershocks.

"God, that was amazing," Jeff gasped, clinging to me.

"Incredible," I agreed. "I don't think I've ever come so hard or so long in my life."

"Me, neither," Jeff said.

Silence between us then, for many long minutes, only the susurrus of the wind and the clatter of branches and the distant twitter of sparrows.

"Anna?" Jeff was rummaging in his pants pocket for the odd bulge I'd noticed.

"Hmmm?"

He lifted up on elbow, his shirt open and draping across one of my bare breasts. His hand was closed around the whatever-it-was. My heart was hammering in my chest, thudding with a sudden rush of nerves brought on by the serious expression on Jeff's face.

"I love you, Anna," Jeff started.

"I love you, too—"

"Hold on, now, sweetheart. Let me finish."

Sweetheart, he'd called me. It made my heart melt and tangle more thoroughly around his.

"I love you, Anna," he started again, as if reciting something he'd memorized. "I know this is maybe a little crazy and a little sudden, but I just know it's right, it's meant to be. I love you too much to ever let you get away again."

I had a sudden flood of panic as I realized what he was leading up to. My eyes stung and burned. My breath caught, and I felt as if time had stopped. The breeze, which had blowing all the time, had gone still, and the even birds were silent.

Jeff opened his hand, showing me, yes, a black box. He opened it with one hand, revealing a slim platinum band topped by a princess-cut diamond, glittering in the sun.

"Will you marry me?"

Shit. Shit shit shit.

I didn't know what to say, what to do, what I was even thinking or feeling. Tears fell unheeded, tears of joy and confusion. I loved him, so much. I wanted to be with him. But...this? Now?

"Anna?"

"Jeff, I—I love you, so much. I do. My heart is saying yes, but—"

"But?" Jeff was puzzled, confused, hurting.

"I'm not saying no, Jeff, I'm not."

"But you're not saying yes."

"I'm saying, can I have some time to think? I mean, this is so sudden, so unexpected. I only want to be with you, and I...I want to say yes, but...I just need a day or two to really think about it."

Jeff nodded slowly. "I guess I get that. But you're...you're not saying no?"

I shook my head and put my hands on his clean-shaven face, kissed him hard and deep. "No, Jeff. I'm not saying no. I just need to process it before I say yes. I don't know if that makes any sense or not, but I just—"

"No, it does. I did sorta spring this on you kind of suddenly. I love you, sweetheart. If you need some time to think, then that's fine by me. Take whatever time you need."

Not long after that, we packed up, the champagne unopened, and left. Jeff seemed quiet, or rather, more subdued than usual. I felt bad, knowing he'd hoped it'd be a joyous occasion, an exuberant yes. I just couldn't give him that, not yet. I hadn't even considered him proposing, not for a long time yet.

We went home, and for the first time in days, we went to sleep without making love.

We had a DJ shift the next day, at, of all places, The Dive. The place where I'd first sang with Chase.

As we unloaded and set up, my gaze went to the alley where I'd first touched and tasted Chase. A pang went through me.

I didn't precisely miss him, per se. He'd been vital to me feeling my own worth. Before him, I'd never thought of myself as beautiful, really. I'd accepted myself, and even liked who I was, but didn't think of myself as an object of male desire. Chase had changed that. He'd shown me men could think I was beautiful. He'd wanted me, he'd shown me in glorious detail what sex could and should be.

Without him, I wouldn't have ever had the courage to approach Jeff.

My thoughts were a whirlwind as we set up and started the first set.

Jeff had proposed. *Proposed.* He wanted to marry me.

But what if I'd been wrong about Chase? What if he'd had real feelings for me, too? If I was being honest with myself, I'd felt things stirring for him, which was part of the reason I'd bolted at the first opportunity. Sex with Chase was great, and he'd given a priceless gift in helping me see my own power as a sexual woman.

What if I'd been wrong? The thought wouldn't go away.

Jeff wants to marry me. Why was I hesitating? I loved him. I knew it, felt it as true deep inside me, in my bones and my blood, in my heart and my mind, in the core of myself as a woman, I knew I loved him. What was more, I trusted Jeff, completely.

We had a dead spot, no one signing up for songs, so I sang, to prompt some requests. I did "Alone" by Heart. It was a song I'd loved pretty much my entire life, and it was something I could perform in my sleep and nail it every time. I knew each note the way I knew my own face in the mirror. It was comforting and familiar when all the rest of me was tumultuous, chaotic, confused.

I stepped outside after my song ended, caught my breath and tried to calm my jangling nerves. When I went back in, Jeff was cueing up a song, a strange, tight expression on his face.

A male figure was standing just off to the side of the stage area. I didn't recognize him at first, since he'd shaved his head and was wearing plain tight blue jeans instead of leather pants, and a tight white T-shirt instead of something flashy and rock star. He turned, mic in hand.

Chase. What the hell is he doing here?

My heart shot into my throat, my fists clenched, my stomach dropped away. If I was confused before, there simply wasn't a word for my emotions when Chase's eyes locked onto me.

He looked good with a shaved head. It set off his eyes, the sharp contours of his gorgeous face.

He'd gauged his ears and had new ink crawling up his forearm.

He didn't smile when he saw me, didn't walk toward me, just stared at me, hard, intense, poised.

The music started, the opening bars of a song I knew all too well: "With or Without You" by U2. Oh, hell. God, he sounded good. He sang the entire song standing sideways on the stage, pinning me in the doorway with his fiery gaze.

I can't live...with or without you...

It was clearly a message, each word spoken directly to me. He was pouring his heart out to me, telling me what was inside him. By the time the song ended, I knew one thing for absolutely certain: I wasn't over Chase Delany.

Oh, god.

Tears were sluicing down my face, chest heaving. The song ended, the music faded, Chase spotlighted on the tiny stage. No one spoke, no one moved, no one even breathed. Everyone was waiting. For what?

Out of the corner of my eye, I saw Jeff standing behind the mixer, a glass of Coke in his hand.

Chase reached into his pocket, pulled out something small and round and glinting in the dim bar light. He held it up, slowly lowered himself to one knee.

No, no no no. Please no. Oh, god, no. Please don't—

Chase spoke into the microphone, his eyes drilling into mine: "Anna, I know this is crazy. We haven't known each other all that long, and I know we had a big misunderstanding. But the thing is, I'm in love with you. I fell in love with you from the very first moment I laid eyes on you. I can't live without you. I want you to come on tour with me. I want us to see the world together.

"Anna, will you marry me?"

The glass in Jeff's hand shattered.

A single sob tore from my throat. I shook my head, turned, and slammed against the crash bar and out into the night.

⟶⋅◦⋅⟵

Turn the page for a sneak peek at *Big Girls Do It Married*, the full-length novel coming soon!

Big Girls Do It Married

I FOCUSED ON BREATHING. Breathe in, clutch the bouquet of roses in trembling fingers; breathe out, one slow step forward. Wide double doors were pulled open from within the chapel, revealing a dozen dark wood pews, filled on both sides of the aisle. Each pew was garlanded at the aisle-end with a bow of white silk and a single pink rose. The aisle itself was covered in pale pink rose petals.

My heart was beating so hard I thought the entire chapel could hear it pounding like a drum. When the doors opened, an older woman with silver hair began Mendelssohn's "Wedding March" on a grand piano. I was shaking so bad the roses trembled in my hands. My knees were weak, my throat thick and burning.

Then I looked up and saw him. He was resplendent in a traditional tuxedo, his eyes wavering with emotion as he watched me. As if sensing my nerves, he smiled at me and mouthed *I love you*. My nerves receded, and I could move again. I'd been rooted to the spot at the doors, Jamie behind me holding my train. Now, with his eyes on me, loving me, I was able to take the first step forward.

The aisle wasn't all that long, but the measured walk from the doors to *him* seemed to take an eternity. With each step, I realized more fully how ready I was for this. I didn't think I would be, even when I agreed to marry him. I worried, all the way up until the moment I saw him at the altar, that I wouldn't be ready. But I was.

I'm ready. I want to do this.

With every step closer to the man I love, I realized that this was exactly what I wanted, and you couldn't have dragged me away from the altar with a thousand wild horses.

At long last, I reached him. A step up, a second, and then his hands were in mine, holding me, steadying me. His eyes burned into mine, the love in his gaze bringing tears of happiness to my eyes.

"Dearly beloved," the minister began, "we are gathered here today to celebrate the blessed union of this man and this woman..."

It really sank in, then, as the minister began his brief sermon:

I'm getting married.

Big Girls Do It Married,
the full-length novel,
is coming soon!

About the Author

JASINDA WILDER is a Michigan native with a penchant for titillating tales about sexy men and strong women. When she's not writing, she's probably shopping, baking, or reading. She loves to travel, and some of her favorite vacations spots are Las Vegas, New York City, and Toledo, Ohio. You can often find Jasinda drinking sweet red wine with frozen berries.

To find out more about Jasinda and her other titles, visit her website: www.Jasindawilder.com.

Made in the USA
Charleston, SC
03 February 2013